Seraph

M.J Palmer

Published by Bone Chilling Publications, 2014

First Edition

A CIP catalogue record for this title is available from the British Library.

Chapter One

New York.
He silently walked along the corridor. This part of the hospital was ominously quiet, devoid of any movement. Elsewhere in the building, there would be a bustle of activity, babies being born, emergency operations taking place, and of course, people dying, but here among the wards there was a deafening silence. Joshua wondered if it was always this quiet or if it had been made so for his convenience.
He climbed the stairs to the second floor and briskly walked to the end of the corridor, where the ward he wanted was. The soles of his trainers squeaked on the tiled floor as he came to a halt outside the swinging doors. He looked through the glass panel; the ward's low lighting consisted of small night-lights. He gave his eyes a second or two to adjust to the dimness within.
The walls appeared to dance with an abundance brightly painted cartoon characters. Beds lined both sides of the ward, twenty in all, and each bed held a little body, each one suffering from cancer.
He scanned the ward, searching for a member of staff but he saw no one. He looked again, knowing that the children would never be left unattended. Then he noticed a bed at the end of the ward screened by curtains. The duty nurse must be seeing to the child, he told himself. Satisfied, he pushed open the door and walked in, stopping at the first bed he came to.
Only a small bald head protruded from the duvet. Without hair to help, it was impossible for Joshua to tell whether the child was male or female. He moved closer, a smile spreading across his face.
Even in sleep, the child seemed aware someone was watching. Its eyes flickered open.
“Hello.” Joshua said. His voice was as gentle as a whisper.
The child rubbed its nose with a small fist.
“What’s your name?” Joshua asked. From the size, Joshua assumed the child’s age was about five or six.
“Kirsty” she answered in a small voice.
“You haven’t been feeling very well, have you Kirsty.”
“No, I’ve got Leukaemia.”

Her matter of fact answer shook him a little. He gave her a full beaming smile. “Tell me Kirsty, would you like to be well again, so you can go home and play with your friends?”
“And would I be able to back to school?” She gave him a weak smile but her eyes shone with joy at the pleasure the thought gave her.
“And go to school,” Joshua assured her. “Kirsty, take my hand and I will make you better.”
Kirsty sat up and held out her hand. Joshua took hold of her tiny, soft, warm hand in both of his. A movement from the next bed caught his eye. The child was awake, watching him.
“Hello, what’s your name?” Joshua’s voice, no more than a whisper carried clearly in the silence.
“Joe.” The boy told him.
Joshua bent down and kissed the palm of Kristy’s hand, then walked over to the boy’s bed. “I was just telling Kirsty that I could make her well again. Would you like me to do the same for you?” asked Joshua.
“No one can make me better. I’m going to die!” said Joe without any emotion.
“Who told you that you were going to die?” Joshua found that statement hard to believe; even if the child were dying, surely they wouldn’t have told him.
“No one…but my mum was crying after she spoke to the doctors. She hasn’t cried since I first became ill, so I guessed I must be dying.”
Joshua was amazed at the children’s acceptance of their own mortality; adults would be fighting savagely to hold onto life in their fear of death.
“Well, how about you take hold of my hand and together we’ll put that smile back on your mother’s face.” He winked at the boy.
“Go on, Joe, take his hand.” Kirsty urged the boy. The warmth from the man’s hand was still wafting through her body, making waves of pure heat, which gave her a glowing feeling deep inside.” It feels great, sort of warm and tingling.”
Joshua gave Kirsty a quick smile, as he went to Joe. He appreciated her description, this being his first chance to use his gift, and he was glad that it was such a pleasant sensation.
Joe took Joshua’s hand and felt the sunshine spread through his veins.

“Wow! How do you do that?” Joe’s eyes widened with wonder.
“Are you a doctor?” A boy in the next bed asked, as he watched.
“And you are?” Joshua asked as he moved on to the next bed. The boy told him his name was Eric. “No, Eric, I’m not a doctor”.
“So how can you make us better if you’re not a doctor?”
“Maybe MAGIC” Joshua laughed, but his voice held a conviction as if he really believed in magic. Kirsty and Joe did, they could feel it.
“There’s no such thing as magic” said Eric, his mouth pouted stubbornly.
“So you won’t want to take my hand.” Joshua held his hand out to the boy. Eric eyed Joshua for a moment or two then smiled and placed his hand in his.
“You’re a very wise young man.” Joshua laughed quietly.
”Mr. Can you make anyone better?” A little girl asked. She still boasted a beautiful head of auburn hair.
“Of course I can, sweetheart, give me your hand.”
“No, it’s not me, it’s my friend.” She pointed towards the bed. “Anna’s my best friend and she is ever so sick. Can you make her better?” Her big green eyes stared at him in awe, as if she had woken to find Santa at the bottom of her bed.
Joshua stared at the curtained bed, wondering if his powers could reach the child without taking her hand. He could try, he decided, and if it wasn’t successful, he could treat her tomorrow. He dare not go any closer to the child, in fear of discovery. He had to treat, as many of the children as possible, one or two wouldn’t be enough to convince them.
He tried to visualise the child, he could hear her being sick, in his minds eye he took her hand in his and allowed the power to flow into her. When he had finished he could still hear her being sick, which didn’t mean anything, for he didn’t know how long it took the power to take effect. He turned to Anna’s friend.
“I’ve done my best, sweetheart, but whether I’ve succeeded or not, I can’t say.” He took her hand and kissed it. “You’re a very special person, Princess.”
He moved on to the next bed. It was as he reached the sixth bed that heard the door swing open.
“What the hell are you doing?” Sister Murray shouted when she saw Joshua leaning over the boy. ”Carol” she called. A nurse’s head

popped out from behind the curtain. "What's this man doing here?" the sister demanded to know.
"Carol stared at Joshua. "I don't know, sister, I've been seeing to Anna." She hadn't known the man was there, but she knew she would get the blame for it.
"Make sure he doesn't get away. I'll call security." The sister ran to the desk and pressed the panic button the switched on the main lights.
"It's alright." Joshua tried to assure her, "I haven't hurt them; in fact I've done the opposite." His voice was low and velvety.
"He's making us better." Kirsty told the sister. "And I can go back to school."
"Yeah, he's not a doctor, he's magic." said Eric.
Within seconds, two security men and a doctor came rushing in.
"I found this man bending over one of the boys. He told the children he was giving them a cure." The sister shuddered to think what the pervert had really been doing.
"I have cured them." Joshua tried to tell them, not that he expected them to believe him.
The two security men grabbed him by the arms, twisted them up his back and started to drag him from the ward.
"Stop it, you're hurting him." Kirsty began to cry. "He's a nice man and you're hurting him." The other children joined in her tears.
"Its okay, Kirsty." Joshua had to speak louder, so that his voice was heard over their crying. "Go to sleep now, you've got a very busy day ahead of you tomorrow, and I will see you in the morning."
"In your dreams, mister." The security man scoffed.
"I'll be back," Joshua said with confidence. "When they realise that I have cured them." He allowed himself to be led away.
"Mister," Joe called. "What's your name?"
"Joshua." He smiled and for a second his eyes flashed with a halo of light.

Chapter Two

Pakefield, Suffolk.
He stepped silently through the dimly lit corridor. The place appeared to be deserted but for him. He stopped outside double doors and peered through the window. Satisfied, he pushed open the door and walked through. Beds lined the room, he walked over to the first, a tiny baldhead was all that poked over the top of the duvet. He grinned down at the child.
"No..." Gemma woke to find herself sitting bolt upright, without a thought she threw back the duvet and jumped out of bed, slipping on her dressing gown a she went. She padded bare footed to the children's bedroom, turning the handle, she pushed open the door, half expecting to see the man from her dream standing over her daughter Laura as she lay sleeping.
Both children were sleeping peacefully. Gemma let out the breathe that she realised she was holding and walked over to Laura's bed, she watched her sleep for a few seconds then ran her hand over her daughter's dark curly locks. A tear crept into the corner of her eye. Laura's hair had grown back thicker and stronger, just as she would grow strong again, Gemma assured herself. Laura let out a sleepy sigh and turned in her sleep. Gemma turned to the other bed where her son Luke slept in his normal fashion, on his belly, an arm and leg hung over the side of the bed. She fought the urge to move him, he always looked so uncomfortable like that, but she knew from experience that if she moved him, he'd be back in the same position within a few minutes, instead she pulled the duvet so that it covered his arm and leg that dangled. She turned to leave the room, allowing herself a final look before closing the door and returning to bed.
"Children all right, Gem?" her husband Thadius asked from the bed.
"Yes, both dead to the world."
As she got back into bed, he pulled her towards him. "Jesus! You're freezing woman." He cried, but held her closer to him, wrapping his arm around her to chase way the chill.
"Sorry, but I had to go and check on them, I had a ...well I suppose it was a dream, the first time I've ever had a dream in my life and it

had to be a bad one. I had to make sure they were okay." She told him of her dream. "I thought it was death coming to take Laura." The words sounded silly now, yet she still felt like she had a block of ice in her stomach.
Thadius lifted her chin so that he could see her face, "Laura will be alright, Gemma." It sounded like a prayer. "The doctors are pleased with her progress, her blood count is back to normal, she's…" he stopped himself from saying (beaten it) you didn't challenge the gods. "She's growing stronger every day. She'll be fine. I promise." However, they both knew it would be years before they'd know whether such promises were kept. They lay silently, both deep in their own thoughts.
"Hey, Happy birthday." His hand trailed from her back, over her hips, down between her inner thighs. "So, do you want your birthday present now." He teased, his fingers caressing her.
"But it's five o'clock in the morning." She laughed.
"So." He rolled over on top of her "It's your birthday."
"Well I hope this isn't all I'm going to get for my birthday," she giggled as he nibbled her neck.
Oh, you'll be pleased with what I've got for you." He breathed, his words holding intimate promise. They kissed passionately, stirring the juices that were so ready to flow.
"Mummy" Laura's voice floated through.
Thadius felt her return to the night. "Leave her, she'll go back to sleep." He said half heartedly, through their kiss. He felt her shift as the voice called again.
She sighed. "No" she gently pushed him away. "It's not fair to her." Thadius sighed and rolled onto his back, knowing he'd lost a battle that he could never win.
"I won't be long." She promised. "It was probably me who disturbed her in the first place." She leaned forward and gave his nipple a sucking bite "and don't you dare go back to sleep." She warned.
"Don't be long." He slapped her bottom playfully as she rolled off the bed and watched as she covered her body with her dressing gown and left the room.

Later that morning Thadius and the children woke her with a breakfast tray and presents. Laura and Luke excitedly helped

Gemma open her presents, then settled down in bed beside her, to munch cold toast and the chocolates they had bought her.

Chapter Three

Gemma was in the kitchen preparing sandwiches when Ben rang at the door.
"Ben" she kissed his cheek. "Come in and I'll make you a cup of tea"
"Is Thadius here?" asked Ben, as he made his way through the door.
"No, he's taken the children to get my birthday cake. They shouldn't be long." She noticed a man standing behind Ben and watched as he came forward.
"Gemma, this is my nephew Jim Harding." Ben introduced them.
The man held out his hand to her. Gemma felt a little shocked. Silly really, but she had never imagined that Ben had any family of his own, he had never mentioned any before, and here he was, bringing a member of it to her birthday tea.
"I hope you don't mind me coming along uninvited, Mrs. Williams, only Ben said you wouldn't." The man said as if he had read her mind.
"Of course I don't mind. Ben knows that any friend of his is welcome. Oh, and my name is Gemma."
Ben was waking into the sitting room, but Jim waited just inside the door, she realised he was waiting for her to lead the way; she passed him, feeing slightly self-conscious of his eyes watching her.
"Jim was hoping to look through the old church records, so I said I'd bring him over to introduce him Thadius." Ben told her as she joined him. Ben had already made himself comfortable in an armchair. He always looked more at home here, than he did in his cottage, even though Thadius and she had taken over the vicarage seven years ago, it still seemed more his home than theirs, whenever he came to visit.
"Well, if you want to take the keys, Ben, you know where to find them." Gemma offered.
"No, I wouldn't dream of it, not without asking Thadius first. It's his church now, besides didn't you threaten a cup of tea?"
"Tad wouldn't mind, you know that."
"Well I would have, when it was my church, so I'll wait. Oh, here's your present," he pulled a small packet from his pocket. "Happy birthday, Gemma."
She quickly tore off the wrapping and opened the box. "Crystal earrings! Oh, they're beautiful, Ben. Where did you find them? I've

looked everywhere and can never find any." She swapped them for the earrings she was wearing and turned her head from left to right, for his approval. The light caught, sending the sparkle dancing.
"They're beautiful, Ben, thank you." She gave him a big hug and a kiss. He laughed.
Jim, who was watching the scene, felt a little uncomfortable and surprised. He was sure this wasn't the normal behaviour between retired vicar and new vicar's wife.
As though reading his mind. "We go back a long way." Ben assured him.
"Ben's my saviour." Gemma mocked, but the love in her eyes, mocked the mockery.
Ben, tutted. "Saviour, indeed. I found her as a baby, one night in my church, abandoned. I handed her over to the authorities, and then I forgot about her."
"I would have died, had you not found me. They reckon I was only a day or two old and the nights are still cold in April. I would have been dead by morning." Gemma saw it as no small feat. He was her hero, father, or as near as she could get to having one and she wasn't going to let him boo-hoo it.
"You were abandoned in his church!" Jim said, his voice sounded incredulous, you read about babies being abandoned but you never thought about what happened to them.
"Yes abandoned to the world and the night and Ben rescued me." Gemma beamed. She had been making Ben cringe like this for year, but she knew he secretly liked it. It was part of the binding, a binding tighter than pure biological ties could be.
She left Ben to answer Jim's questions, while she made the tea, returning in time to hear Ben tell Jim that he gave no more thought to her.
"Abandoned again." She released a heavy sigh, as she joined them.
"Yes and she has been using that line ever since she knew what it meant." Ben chided.
"You have to use everything that you can in this life." She laughed.
"So what happened?" Jim asked genuinely interested. "You must have worried—hence the relationship."
"No, I met Gemma again four or five years later, I thought purely by accident but later I realised it was some sort of penance. No, a couple in my congregation were killed in a car accident, leaving two

young sons. It was them that I went to see at the orphanage." He took a sip of tea before continuing. "The orphanage was in my parish, but to my shame, I had very little dealing with it, apart from raising money for it along with the other local charities. When the Johnston boys went there, I thought it my duty to visit them. Once there, Mrs Slater, the woman who ran the home, wasn't going to let me escape so easily."
"Poor woman, she had the hots for Ben for years, but he never succumbed to her womanly wiles. Although we did used to wonder about them, as we got older." Gemma interrupted.
"Gemma!" Ben cried. When he was sure she was going to say no more on the subject he went on." Mrs Slater asked if I could give some of the younger children religous instruction.
She said that the elder children came to church every Sunday but that she didn't think it would be appreciated if she brought along thirty odd younger ones." He finished his tea and Gemma automatically refilled his mug.
"So I arranged to hold a special service at the church, that week, especially for the younger children. I can tell you, I was feeling rather good about myself when I returned to the orphanage a couple of days after the service. As the saying, goes pride comes before a fall. I was telling Mrs Slater how well I thought the service had gone and that we might make it a regular event, when she started laughing. I was a bit taken back, she apologised and explained that one little girl wouldn't agree, she had told Mrs Slater that she wasn't going there again, as God didn't even say hello he just hid behind a curtain all the time, and she didn't even get a cup of tea," He glared at Gemma as she laughed. Although they had told their story many times, they enjoyed it none the less.
"It wasn't my fault, one of the women who looked after us, had been making us all excited for day. Telling us that we had to be on our best behaviour when we went to God's house, that he wouldn't like it if we were naughty. We all thought that we were going to someone's house for tea, we were all disappointed, but I was the only one who said anything."
"I had to laugh." Ben smiled as he remembered. "I said I had better try to explain things to her. I asked who the child was, and she told me it was the baby I had found in my church. She said her name was Gemma Stephens, which they had named after my church St.

Stephens. She took me to the garden and brought Gemma to me. I spent quite a while trying to explain as simply as I could, about the church, Jesus and God. All the time she listened without saying a word. At the end of it, I still wasn't sure she understood, so I asked her if there was anything she wanted to ask me. She looked up at me, with those big green eyes and said. Are you my daddy?" Ben roared with laughter.
"Some of the older children had been teasing me, about my mother not wanting me and giving me to the vicar. I was upset, so Mrs Slater told me what happened, and then a day later Ben came along to talk to me, I thought he had come to claim me. I was quite upset when he said he wasn't my dad." Gemma explained.
"Well that was it, I was enchanted. I didn't stand a chance after that. You see, I had never really thought much about children, or the joy that they could bring. My wife had died young, before we had any children and I knew I would never remarry, so no child would ever call me daddy, then this little thing, who had no one, had and it touched my heart. Therefore, I became father figure to her. Not that it was always a pleasure; Gemma was a bit of a tear-away. Mrs Slater was always asking me to have a word with her about no thing or another."
"They used to blackmail me with him. It was always, we'd have to tell Reverend Mason if you don't stop doing such a thing. It wasn't easy growing up with a vicar for a hero, you know" Gemma told him.
"As I remember things, I always had to get you out of trouble; you defiantly weren't scared of me. She even used to quote me to the teachers, completely out of context, to try to get her out of trouble. Until one of the teachers told me I was making a rebel out of her."
"I was never a rebel; I just used to stick up for myself. I was never bad."
""No, never bad," Ben smiled. "Strong willed and fiery, but never bad."
"Well, you seemed to have enjoyed it." Jim concluded. "I suppose you met your husband through Ben."
"No, that was nothing to do with me; Gemma spotted him In Lowestoft, on his way here, and decided he was the man she was going to marry. She only came o me to find out who he was. If anything, I tried to discourage them. I didn't think Thadius was the

right sort of man for her, he seemed far too serious, I was afraid he would snuff out that spark she has. I needn't have worried, she changed him." Ben smiled
"It was your fault, Ben, you taught me to see the man behind the dog collar. Besides Tad was never serious, he was just scared of you, what with being new to the profession as well."
"I must confess I didn't take their relationship too seriously, I didn't believe that a vicar would marry an atheist." Ben laughed, but Jim believed he heard a serious dig there.
"Maybe Tad saw the woman behind the atheist, besides I'm not an atheist, I'm just not sure that I believe in what the Bible says, that's all. Tad understands, we don't discuss it anymore, because he takes it as a personal attack, but I go to church every week,"
"You have no faith." Ben accused
"I have faith," she said quietly. "I believe in Tad and you."
A brooding silence gaped between them. Jim wished he had never brought up the subject, it was time he changed it. "How old are your children?" He asked just for something to say.
"Four, they're twins, Laura and Luke." She smiled an apology.
"How is Laura?" Ben asked in a tight voice, regretting what he'd said before.
"Fine," she smiled "She gets stronger every day." She remembered her dream and her blood ran cold through her veins, she wondered why a dream should have such an effect on her, but now wasn't the time to ponder. She heard a key turn in the front door lock. "That sounds like them now."
"Granddad." Laura and Luke called as they saw Ben. "We've been out buying mummy's cake."
"I hope it isn't a teddy bear." Ben laughed.
"No, you're safe this year we got one with flowers." Thadius laughed as he came through the door. "Hello, Ben."
"I'm bigger now, Granddad." Laura said her lips pouting. Luke and her father had been teasing her all morning about the scene she had made last year.
"They bought a teddy bear cake last year, but we couldn't eat it because Laura started to cry as soon as we went to cut it up." Been explained the joke to Jim. "Thadius, this is my nephew, Jim Harding, he's a genealogist and he'd like to go through the church records some time." Ben introduced them. The two men shook hands.

"That's if it's no trouble." Jim said.
"No of course it isn't. When did you want to look at them?"
"Anytime, I'm staying for a week, so whenever it's convenient for you."
"Well come over anytime, if I'm not here Ben and Gemma know where to find them."
"Can we have a piece of cake now?" Luke asked.
"Yes, hoggychops." She tickled her son's stomach. "There's sandwiches and jelly as well, don't forget."
"We can have cake first though, can't we?" Laura joined in.
"Come on then, you can help me lay the table." Gemma treated everyone birthday, as a party for the children, they enjoyed tea parties so much. She could hear Thadius, Ben and Jim chatting about Jim's work as she and the children prepared the table. She loved times like this, with her family around her. What more could anyone want for their birthday? She asked herself.

Chapter Four

Joshua looked towards the cell door as he heard the key turn in the lock. "I take it the hospital has been in touch." Joshua said to the detective who had spent the early hours of the morning questioning him.
"This way, Mr Powell." The detective ignored the man's question. He had no choice but to release the creep, the orders had come from the top, but it didn't mean he had to be civil to the man. He had spent hours questioning this pervert, only to listen to his crazy ravings of how he had cured the kids and how in the morning the police would know the truth. Many times during those long hours of questioning, Sergeant Fuller had wanted to hit this man, just to take that silly smile off his face. He would have done, as well, if his partner Bob hadn't been there. Bob reckoned Powell was just a harmless nutter, but as Fuller told him, there was no such thing as a nutter being harmless. Bob reckoned they'd get more out of the man if they humoured him, so Fuller let Bob take over questioning him.
"Right, Mr Powell." Bob had begun.
"Call me Joshua, Please." Joshua smiled.
Fuller laughed his anger, but a stern look from Bob made him back off.
"Right Joshua," Bob went on. He had the patience of a saint. "You say you went to the hospital to heal the children." Joshua smiled his agreement.
"Right," Bob went on in his easy way. "But why at midnight, wouldn't t have been better to have gone in the daytime, so that you wouldn't have disturbed their sleep?"
"Disturbing their sleep doesn't seem that important when you're healing them." He heard Fuller grunt. He held up a hand to him. "Please, sergeant, allow me to explain. I understand your questions, you think it a strange time to go to the children, but the explanation is quite simple. The power to heal was a birthday gift from my father. Bestowed upon me at a second past midnight. Well I couldn't wait to start my work; there are so many children dying, so many children in the world that I have to heal. However, it's all right, I don't resent you wasting my time with your questions. I understand you're only concerned with the children's well being, but tomorrow

the truth will be known. Then I will be able to continue my father's work."
"Jesus." Fuller swore from where he stood in the corner. Joshua turned to look at him and smiled. For a moment, Fuller had thought he had seen a light flash in the man's eyes. He turned away from his smiling face.
"So how do you heal the children, is it hard, what do you have to do to them?" Bob feigned interest. He'd rather hear what this creep did to the children from him, than hear it first hand from the kiddies.
"It isn't hard at all. I only have to make contact with the children to allow the power to pass through me to them."
Bob wondered, what this thing he called the power was. He chased the thought from his mind. "So you just touch the children. Where do you touch them, does it have to be a certain place you touch?"
"No, I…wait a minute, sergeant, you've been in this job too long, it's warped your mind or perhaps you've always hand an evil mind and that's why you joined the police force…I hold the children's hands, sergeant, nothing else. One of the children, Anna, I think the girl said her name was, was being treated so I couldn't get near her so I tried to cure her by thought alone, whether or not I was successful, I don't know but the other six are cured. The doctors will find that out in the morning."
"All right, I've heard enough of this crazy, lock him up, Bob." Fuller had said at last.
They had learnt nothing. The man Powell was from Australia. (It was a shame he hadn't stayed there) Fuller grumbled. They had enough of their own nutters. They had checked with the Australian police, but he had no record there. They would have to talk with the children in the morning, the hospital said they'd let them know when the kids were ready for questioning. Luckily, that wouldn't be their job.
When the call came through, it hadn't been what Fuller had expected. Joshua Powell was to be released and escorted back to the hospital.
He stood now, holding the car door open for the man to get in.
"Don't worry, Sergeant, I forgive you for your evil thoughts." Joshua told him as he got in the car.

There it was again, that flash of light in his eyes, like a halo of light around the edge of his iris, there for a second or two then it was gone.
Fuller only had to hand him over to a Dr. Cummings and it wouldn't be a second too soon, as far as he was concerned, the man gave him the creeps.
When they met the doctor, Joshua asked. "The girl Anna, has he been healed? I couldn't touch her, you see."
"Yes, Anna is well. That's what we want to talk to you about, Mr. Powell. The children claim..." the doctor noticed the police officer.
"Thank you, officer, your assistance will no longer is required."
Fuller was glad to be dismissed.

Chapter Five

Dr. Cummings studied the man. He wasn't sure what he had expected, but Joshua wasn't it. He hadn't really given it a lot of thought, what with everything going on, but from the way the children had spoken about Joshua, this morning; he had expected him to be bigger, awe inspiring with a personality that demanded respect. The children definitely had all the signs of devotion, just the mention of his name seemed to mesmerise them, their eyes sparkled with admiration as they told him what Joshua had said and how they had felt when he touched their hands. Little Mary Smith absolutely shone when she told him Joshua had called her princess.
He smiled to himself; children had a way of seeing people differently from adults. Joshua was no different from any other man his age, a little scruffier than most perhaps, but that might have been contributed to by his night in a cell, about thirty, his dark brown hair hung straight to his shoulders, his fringe and full beard allowed only his brown eyes and a broken nose to make up his face, 5' 10" in height, he was no different from any other man. Except of course, that he had told six children that they would be cured of their cancer by morning and seven children appeared to have been cured. He said appeared, because there were many more tests to be run, but by the looks of the children, this morning, it was hard to believe that they had ever had a day's illness in their lives, let alone cancer the night before.
At first, they hadn't taken the children's stories seriously, thinking that some nutter had managed to get to the children without being stopped by security. He had expected heads to roll, including his, for allowing such a thing to happen. However, when Joseph McKenna's blood test came back normal, he wondered, and then dismissed the notion, instead he blamed the nurse for getting the blood samples mixed up. Not wanting any more trouble than he would already get, he took another sample himself and took it to the lab so there could be no mistake. When that also came back normal and the children insisted that it was just as Joshua said it would be he had every child on the ward tested. Seven of the children's results came back normal, even Anna Bailey, whom they were expecting to lose over the next couple of days, appeared no longer to have cancer.

He had called in other doctors, all experts in this field. Those doctors were now waiting in his office to meet his man, desperate to ask questions, having run their own tests and coming to the same conclusions as his own, that seven of the twenty children appeared not to have cancer and never had, although their medical records proved otherwise.
Cummings realised that the man Joshua was looking at him, he pulled his thought together. "I'm sorry, Mr Powell." He held his hand out to the man, and then consciously withdraws it. "Allow me to introduce myself, I'm Dr. Cummings."
Joshua took the doctor's withdrawn hand and shook it. "Please call me Joshua."
Dr. Cummings smiled his embarrassment, what had he expected to happen on taking the man's hand, he chided himself. "If you will follow me to my office. My colleagues and I have many questions we'd like to ask you, Mr...Joshua."
"No, first we go to the children, your questions can wait." Joshua said as he turned to walk away.
Shocked, the doctor followed him up to the children's ward, stopping only to instruct a nurse to ask the doctors in his office to join him on the ward.
As they reached the ward, a scream of glee from the children greeted them. Seven children ran to him, their faces shining, expectant as if he was bearing gifts.
"Joshua, those horrible men let you go, they didn't hurt you, did they?" Kristy's face frowned with concern.
"I told you not to worry," his eyes danced with light as he smiled down at Kirsty. "I said I'd be back. So how are you all feeling this morning?"
"Great!" they all cheered unanimously.
"No more talk of death. Joey?"
"No." the boy laughed.
"Ha, Princess, how's my special girl this morning?"
Mary only smiled shyly; she was in love.
"Excuse me, Mr...Joshua, my baby, she's only two, please could you help her, and she's a good girl and..."
"That's what I'm here for." He assured the mother.
All hell broke out then, as parents tried to lead him to their child first. Joshua held his ground.

“Paul,” he looked around for the boy. “You were the last one I met last night, where’s your bed?”
“Here, Joshua.” He ran and jumped on his bed.
”Then we shall continue from there.” He made his way through the children and parents. He saw a little girl holding Mary’s hand; her eyes stared largely at him, a little afraid. He squatted down in front of her. “You must be Anna; we didn’t have the opportunity to meet last night. I’m Joshua.” He held his hand out to the girl, who was cured this morning along with the other six, although she hadn’t seen the man, she had been told all about him by her best friend Mary.
“Hello,” her voice was quiet.
“It’s a pleasure to meet you, Anna, you didn’t sound very well last night, and I hope you’re feeling better now.” She nodded her reply.
“Good. Now if you will excuse me, I have a lot of work to do.”
Joshua went to the bed next to Paul’s, he asked the boy his name and held his hand , then moved on to the next bed. By the time, he reached the fourth bed, the mother of the first child cried. “He seems better already.”
“Yes, the healing is immediate.” Joshua assured the parents.
“But, Joshua, you said we had to wait until morning.” Eric accused Joshua, as if he felt himself to have been ill-treated.
Joshua laughed. He liked this cheeky little boy. “That’s because you needed your sleep.” He ran a finger down Eric’s nose playfully. He worked his way down the other side of the ward.
When he had treated all the children, the doctors asked him how he cured the children. “I asked my father for the gift, not how it worked.” Was his only answer.
“Is it only cancer you can cure, Joshua?” asked a young doctor, who had come down from another ward, wanting to see the man for himself, after hearing what was happening.
“No, I can heal all children from all life threatening diseases and all disabilities.” He smiled at the doctor, knowing why the doctor had asked.
The young doctor disappeared. Returning a couple of minutes later with a child of about ten, in a wheelchair, who was brain damaged.
“This is Louise, she’s been severely brain damaged since she had complications from measles when she was a year old.” Dr Coull had an affinity with the child, she being one of his first patients, as a student doctor. “Can you help her?”

Tears misted in Joshua's eyes as he looked at the child. Her head continuously moved from side to side, as it lay against the headrest; her eyes stared without any recognition of what she saw. A mewling sound issued from her mouth and saliva dribbled, painfully, over her red, sore chin. Her arms and hands spasmodically jerked and contorted, uncontrollably.
Joshua knelt down in front of her, dabbed her chin softly with her bib. He gentle stroked the girls face. In a hushed voice, he said. "Hello, sweetheart, I think it's time you were awakened from your sleep, don't you, Louise?" He took her hand in his and spoke silently to himself as if in prayer.
Slowly the girl stopped her spasmodic movement. She looked at peace as she lifted her head from the headrest, her eyes sparkling towards Joshua.
"She'll need a good teacher." Joshua told the doctor.
"We've got one, a very good one."
Louise's gaze left Joshua's face and she turned to the voice she knew so well, seeing Dr. Coull she smiled.
"She obviously knows you." Joshua laughed.
"I never realised." He gave Louise's hand a squeeze. "We've a lot of work in front of us, Louise. I just hope you'll still like me at the end of it." He turned his attention back to Joshua. "I have many patients like Louise, can you help them?"
"I can only heal the children." Joshua warned.
Dr Coull looked as though he was going to question this but changed his mind. "I have many children." He smiled. "Can I ask a question, Joshua, what determines a child, physical or mental age?"
Joshua ignored the question. "Lead the way, doctor."
So, Joshua spent his birthday.

Chapter Six

Joshua wearily pushed himself up from the chair; he hadn't had any sleep for the past four days. There were so many children to see, too many children in pain. At least he would be able to sleep on the plane.
"Joshua, you can't leave. We've arranged for specialists from all over the world to bring their own patients for you to treat. You agreed that if your ability to heal was to be proven, it would have to be properly documented by respected doctors who couldn't be doubted." Dr. Cummings panicked.
"Get your specialists over here; I'll be back in time for them. Alan are you ready?" Joshua had asked Alan Coull to join him. Over the past few days, the young doctor had proved his worth, and he didn't ask questions. Joshua could heal the children and that was all the answers he needed.
They made their way to the door of the boardroom where Dr. Cummings had set up the meeting.
"But where are you going?" Dr. Cummings asked.
"Where my father's work sends me." Was the only answer Joshua would give? He had no fondness for Cummings; he seemed to believe he had some control over what was going on. "I'll be back." Joshua repeated as he left. He didn't say when. He wasn't sure how long it would take.
Eric's father was arranging transport. He had introduced himself, two days ago while Joshua was taking one of his rare breaks to eat.
"Joshua, I'm Edward Newton, you cured my son Eric."
"Eric, yes, he's a nice boy, won't you sit down and join me, Mr Newton."
"I had to come and thank you personally, Joshua, although that seems insufficient."
"No thanks are necessary." Joshua assured him. "I do my father's work, that's what I'm here for."
"Yes, I understand that. I asked Dr Cummings if I could pay you for your services but," he rushed on stalling Joshua's protests. "But he said you refused any money, so I won't insult you by offering you any. I know no amount of money could repay you for my son's life. Nevertheless, I am rather wealthy and not without certain influence,

if there is anything I can do for you, you only have to say the word. I could build you clinics, worldwide, where children could come to receive your healing powers. Anything, Joshua, you only have to say the word." Edward Newton needed to do something. He had never owed anybody for anything before in his life and he didn't like the feeling of being beholden to anybody, especially this man.
"I need to get to Africa." Joshua told him.
"I can have my private jet ready for you within two hours." He pulled out his mobile phone and punched in three numbers before Joshua could stop him.
"In a day or two, Mr Newton, I have things to finish here first." So it had been arranged for the jet to be ready today.
Joshua and Alan walked through the lobby to where Newton's limousine was waiting. As they left the hospital, a mob of reporters and parents of the children he had healed confronted them.
"Joshua, is it true, that you have cured children of cancer, just by touching them?" A microphone appeared in front of his mouth.
"Where do you get your powers from, Joshua?"
"Do you have any medical training, Joshua?"
"Why did you choose New York, instead of your native Australia to perform your Miracles?"
The questions were coming thick and fast, but Joshua ignored them and continued walking to the car.
Alan wasn't so in control of himself, he felt confused, with so many people around. He hadn't been outside the hospital since meeting Joshua, or given much thought to what the outside world would think of Joshua's miracles. Questions were now being asked of him.
"Dr Coull, we understand Joshua has cured some of your patients. Can you prove that the children Joshua claims to have cured were actually ill in the first place?" Alan froze, too much was going on for his brain to catch up and tell him what he should be doing.
A hand pulled at his arm. "Come on, Alan, we have work to do." Joshua pulled him to the car. Alan smiled, thankful he was back to reality he could at least understand, he walked on without encouragement.
The limousine's door was open for them. Joshua bent to get in.
"Miracles! Joshua, or some fantastic cruel con trick?" A television reporter accused.

Joshua stood up, a flash of light haloed his eyes, as he glared at the man, and then the light was gone, replaced with a smile.
"Still here, Thomas?" The words were spoken softly, yet were heard clearly by everyone over the commotion, the words rang loudly in their ears, as the crack of an ice-float breaking up in the artic, rings out. Followed by a moment of silence, so deadly, the reporter backed away. Joshua got in the car followed by Alan. The photographers pushed forward again, trying to get one last shot, as the car pulled away.
David Lewis stared after the car. "Bastard." He swore. "The fucking bastard."
His camera operator switched off the camera. He had been waiting for Dave to sign off, but it was obvious that wasn't going to happen, which was probably just as well judging by his face. He had never seen Dave look so angry before and they'd been working together for two years. "Dave, do you want to do the sign off now?" the camera operator asked.
"What? No, fuck it." He was still staring up the road, where the car had disappeared from view. "Did you see what the bastard did, Sam?"
Sam looked a little lost, so Joshua got Dave's name wrong, it was no big deal. That's the problem with being in front of the camera; you started to believe in your own importance. Dave was walking over to their car, it didn't look as if he was going to do the sign-off, but still, that was his problem. Sam packed away the camera and joined him.
"I'll get the little shit; no one uses Dave Lewis and gets away with it." A shade of colour started to return to his face. "Here, you can drive, Sam, I need to think."
Sam caught the keys that were thrown to him. "You should have done the sign-off." Sam moaned.
Dave didn't answer; he was too busy trying to work out what had happened. Why he had felt so scared? The man had only looked at him and said three words, so why did he feel as though he had a pistol put in his mouth, then warned not to sweat. He had worked in war zones, with fucking great big bombs going off around him, and he had never felt so scared, as he did under Joshua's gaze.
Well you picked the wrong person to try to frighten off, mate, the whole world knows you are coning and I'm going to be the man to prove it. He promised himself silently.

“Bastard” He said again.

Chapter Seven

"I thought you might like a sandwich and some coffee." Gemma said as she placed a tray down in front of Jim. Both Thadius and she had been busy all morning, so Jim had been left in the church by himself. She had given him a key to the vicarage, before leaving this morning, and told him to make himself a drink when he wanted one, but on returning she had found he hadn't, so she had taken some over.
"Thanks. Gemma, that's very kind of you." Jim stretched himself as he got up. He picked up the coffee pot and started to pour. "You're not joining me?" he asked when he saw only one cup.
"No, I didn't want to disturb your work."
"I'd be grateful for the disturbance every now and then. I sit there getting too involved and I find that hours have gone by and I've not moved a muscle. It plays havoc with my bones."
"Is it interesting work?" Gemma hoped her voice hadn't betrayed her thoughts, as she couldn't think of anything more boring than riffling through old papers.
"It can be a bit boring at times." He laughed as if he had read her mind. "No, I enjoy it. I get quite a sense of achievement, once I've traced a family right back and it's interesting to see how a family can change."
"And you can make a living out of it?" Gemma always thought it was a thing people did as a hobby.
He smiled. "Quite a comfortable one, thank you."
"Oh, sorry I didn't mean it that way, it's just that I wouldn't have thought that many people were interested in their ancestors." She seemed to be saying all the wrong things.
"You'd be surprised. I've got nothing booked after this, but that's a rarity. I get a fair amount of work through solicitors, but that's usually straight forward, nothing they couldn't do themselves if they had the time and inclination. Mostly it's people who just want to know their origins."
"Just as well there's not more people like me around, or you'd be out of a job." She laughed.
"They never found any clues as to your mother's identity?"

"No, they did all the normal things at the time, you know, television, newspapers, hospitals, doctors and social services." She gave her shoulders a shrug. "I used to think Ben must have known who she was, but no. She was probably just some young girl who was too scared to tell anyone she was pregnant."
"Doesn't it bother you, not knowing?" He couldn't imagine what it must feel like, not to know who you are, not to belong. Some people think families are nothing but trouble and choose not to have anything to do with them, but they had that choice.
"If I said I didn't want to know who my mother was, I'd be lying. Every year, around my birthday, I think, she must be thinking about me, wondering what I'm like, it's only natural. Then I think, maybe she doesn't need to wonder, perhaps she knows, perhaps she lives locally and sees me almost every day. Nevertheless, it isn't that important. I'm not that bothered anymore."
"It must be strange though, not knowing who you are."
"I know who I am. I probably know more about who I am than most people." She spoke a little too strongly. "Most people are told from an early age, oh, you get that from so and so, or you take after, whomever, for that. Well not me, I am who I am."
"So you can't blame anyone else for your horrible characteristics." He tried to lighten her mood.
"I don't have any." She smiled. "No, but seriously, it doesn't bother me. I have my own family now, of course, there is Ben, and Thadius has quite a large family. That's all the family I need. Anyway, I'd better leave you to get on with your work. Will you be here for much longer?"
"A while yet, but if you want me out of here I can come back tomorrow."
"Oh no, I wasn't trying to get rid of you. I thought if your still here later you might like to join us for dinner. I could give Ben a call to see if he wanted to come over."
"That would be nice. Thank you."
"Come over when you're finished then."
"Right, thanks"
Gemma left him to his work.

Later when Jim reached the vicarage, Ben was already there, cocooned in a big comfortable looking armchair. His arms encircling

Luke and Laura, a book held open between them. His voice was bringing the words magically alive, for the joy of the two young eager minds.
The television spoke quietly to itself, having lost it's audience to an old man and the intrigue of a good story.
"Oh, you're here at last." Six eyes looked up at him. "We were beginning to think we'd have to shift you with a crowbar. You'd better let Gemma know you're here." Ben greeted him
"Don't let me disturb the story." He smiled, but realised he'd already lost their attention.
He found Gemma in the kitchen. "Anything I can do to help?" he asked by way of announcing his arrival.
"No. it's all done. Oh, you can tell Thadius I'm dishing up now, he's in the study." She indicated the door opposite.
Jim gave a small tap on the door before entering, strangely feeling like a naughty schoolchild as he stood in silence waiting for Thadius to look up from the paper he held in his hand. He wondered if Thadius was aware of his presence, his concentration so fiercely on the paper, a deep frown creased between his eyebrows.
Suddenly, as if becoming aware of Jim's stare, Thadius looked up, a smile vanished all sings of the frown. "Sorry, Jim, did you want me?"
"Gemma is dishing up." He passed on the message.
"Oh right." He let the paper in his hand fall to the desk. "I'm afraid I lose track of time while I'm writing my sermon." He gave a grimace to the paper. "Not that it gets any better the longer I work on it." He let out a heavy sigh.
"Yes, I suppose it must take quite a talent to constantly bring renewed interest to old stories." Ouch! Perhaps that didn't come out the way he had meant it to; still thankfully, Thadius appeared not to have taken any offence.
"That's the trouble," he smiled ruefully, "my sermons are boring." He said it without shame. "It seems the more thought I put into the words, the more feeling I lose."
"Perhaps you shouldn't write a sermon, just get up there and preach" Jim suggested helpfully.
"Don't, please!" Thadius interrupted with mock alarm. "It's only this piece of paper that allows me to get up there in the first place,

without it I'd babble incoherent like a gibbering idiot. A form of stage fright." Thadius explained.
"A vicar with stage fright." Jim laughed aloud.
"A well kept professional secret, inflicted on many in the clergy."
"Sorry," he said. "I've just never thought of." He laughed again.
"It's the importance of the words, you see, it's only words we can use to convey the understanding of the love and joy that God bestows on mankind. If it was feeling like I was passing on, I am sure they would all understand the peace I feel. However, I only have words at my disposal, and for my sins, I let my congregation down. I'm afraid my parishioners deserve a better man than I."
"You seem to care, what more could anyone ask for?"
"A sermon that doesn't bore them rigid." Thadius laughed. "How about you, how has your day been, did you find what you were looking for.?"
"Yes, it's going quite well."
"Sorry I couldn't be any help to you, this morning. But I'll be here all day tomorrow, so if you need my help just shout. Is Ben here yet?"
"Yes, he's reading Noddy" to the children and I think he's enjoying the story more than they are."
"Probably, but don't we all." said Thadius, remembering his own joy at renewing his acquaintance with the long forgotten childhood friends, as he read to his children.
"I'll tell Ben diner is ready." Jim volunteered, but found them already getting up.
"Look, granddad, It's Jesus." said Laura.
Jim looked at the child in surprise, but saw that she was looking at the television. He followed her gaze to the screen; it was the first news report on Joshua.
"Yes," Ben glanced at the TV. "He does look a little like Jesus doesn't he," he agreed. "Now come on before your mother starts shouting." Ben turned her from the screen.
"He is Jesus." Laura said sulkily as she followed Ben from the room.
"Of course he's not Jesus." Luke started to argue with his sister. "You're being silly."
Jim had to smile.

Chapter Eight

Mike Dune felt depressed. This assignment was useless, nothing was ever going to change for these people, and they were born to die too young. This was his fourth visit in two years, to this living graveyard and nothing had changed, only the people. Yet, he had never renewed an acquaintance from a previous visit, well apart from the relief workers. Many of them had been here for more than two years, how they did it day in and day out was beyond him.
He would be there for a week, maybe longer, and it would take him months to get over the sights and the smells, not that he could ever forget them, how could he, but he had learnt to put such thoughts into a tiny corner of his mind, how else could he survive.
The relief workers always welcomed him like an old friend, giving him and his crew the VIP treatment, which only added to his shame, making him feel more of a fraud.
He had once tried telling Dr Frazer how he felt. Now she was one hell of a woman, twenty-eight years old and she had given up a comfortable little practice in the south east of London in exchange for this god-forsaken place. Leaving behind family and friends to live here, in the belief that her being here, might give some black starving skeleton of a baby one extra day of life. A battle that couldn't be won, no matter how long they fought the war.
She had been very kind to him, telling him that what he did was very important, that more relief came in after he and the rest of the news team showed the plight of these people to the world.
He had wanted to tell her that what he did made no difference. That the people of the world didn't want to know. Figures proved that most people switched to another channel when these reports came on, turning back only when they had finished. But he didn't have the heart.
She had told him that the trick was, not to dwell on all that you're not doing, but to focus on the little that you were. Babies were surviving, that was what was important.
Her smile had been thin, showing the sadness behind it, but sadness was a luxurious emotion that had no place here.
He watched as men carried away the dead, the ones that had been too weak to fight through another day. "So many people, so many…" his

voice trailed off. So many people dying, for the want of a grain of rice.
The people at home resented him, for bringing these pictures into their home, the reality being too horrific. They didn't want to watch children dying, and that was what they were doing every time the camera showed them a child, preferring to close their minds to it, believing it wasn't happening if they didn't see it.
Not bad people, most would take in a stray animal that they didn't really want rather than let it go hungry, but this was too big, too real for their sanity. Think about it and they wouldn't be able to survive. Forget it, think about other things, things they could live with, their own problems, most of them fighting to keep their jobs, a roof over their heads, seeing that their families were well and happy. Forget, how else could they carry on with their lives, go to churches and get solace from their God.
It was not up to them who lived or died, that was the decision of a higher being.
Mike knew this was how most people thought, because they were the same thought as his, his own way of holding on to his sanity. "God, why does life have to be like this?" he swore to himself.
"Mike, are you all right?" Dr Frazer asked the reporter, she had been watching him stare at the people for twenty minutes. "Have you eaten, Mike?" she asked, already knowing the answer, most people could not eat when they first got here, which was stupid, they were here to help these people and you could not help anyone if you were ill, you could only die with them.
"Yes, Julie, I have and you can check with Alex, if you don't believe me." He lied, not being able to keep his stomach steady enough yet to be able to put food in it.
"You will be filming the hospital and the orphanage, won't you, Mike? Only it's important for the people back home can see the good their money can do. We don't want them thinking that it's a hopeless situation, because it's not, so many of these people survive." She tried to make her words optimistic, as she knew how he suffered.
"All arranged a few more days here, then the last two slots on what happens to the people that leave here. Is that the sort of thing you want?"

“Thanks, Mike that will be great.” She stood on tiptoes and kissed his cheek. “I had better get back to work.” She told him and walked away.
Mike followed her with his eye. Such a little thing, he mused, she looked as if a strong wind would knock her over but that little frame of hers held hidden strength, he had seen her working day and night without any sleep, when new arrivals came, she just carried on, always with her sunny outlook. If there were, any justice in this world people would survive on her love alone.
“Don’t thank me, lady; I’m not the one that deserves it.” He said to her disappearing form. He let out a heavy sigh. “Right Mike Dunne stop feeling sorry for yourself, you’ve got work to do.” He scolded himself. Just because they had ousted yesterdays report for some other story didn’t mean he could give up.
He laughed, incredulously; he had learnt this morning that the authorities had decided to throw out his report in favour of a story about some bloke who is supposed to have cured some children of cancer just by touching them. They had assured him that his report would go out today though, as the miracle; man had disappeared, leaving America for destinations unknown.
Mike could just imagine the newspaper headlines in England today. (Do you know where this man is? Find Joshua and so much reward will be yours.) “Welcome to the real world.” He said aloud.

As Mike and his crew got ready to start filming, the children who were feeling well enough started to gather around, the appeal of appearing on television being as strong in them as it was with any children, even though none of these children had ever seen a television set.
“Right, Mike, we’ll just do a sound check,” said Kevin but even as he spoke his attention was being diverted to a jeep, its wheels threw up a cloud of dust from the parched ground as it drew near.
They all watched as the jeep stopped, two men climbed out and walked to the back of the jeep, they started lifting out containers, four in all, each container stood about three foot by two.
Dr. Evans was the first person to reach them and after the initial few words, it was obvious by the doctor’s body language that they were arguing. The news-team went over to find out what was going on.

By the time they reached them, the two men from the jeep were arguing between themselves.
“He’s right, Joshua, let them take the food and put it with the rest, then it can be distributed evenly.” One man implored his companion.
“I’ve come to feed the children; each person will have one item from each container. Now will you help me Alan?” The man said calmly.
“But, Joshua, I thought we’d come to heal the children, but this…this is cruel, Joshua, how can we decide who should eat and who should go hungry.”
“It isn’t for you or me to decide who should eat and who go hungry. Have faith, Alan.” The words were spoken gently.
Alan looked uncomfortable but started to remove the lids from the containers.
The children who had followed the news-crew gathered around the two men and four containers.
Joshua smiled down at the children “You must form a queue.” He told them “otherwise you might miss out. There’s plenty for everyone.” Amazingly, the children behaved brilliantly. “Doctor, we’ll need help.” Joshua told Dr Evans.
“It’s your show, get on with it.” The doctor snarled and walked away to get help to stop this farce.
Perhaps it was because the man’s name was Joshua and the other man had spoken of healing the children, that made Mike wonder, or perhaps he was just so sick of feeling useless and he wanted to do something constructive, or perhaps it was this man’s conviction, whatever Mike found himself saying. “I’ll help.”
“Welcome aboard, brother.” Joshua shook his hand.
As Mike came closer he saw that the first container held small loaves, the second, pieces of cheese, the third fruit and the fourth some sort of rice. He wondered if this man was insane, a thought that was soon lost as hungry hands reached out for the food.
Within minutes, the containers were half-empty. Mike didn’t want to think about what would happen when the food ran out, as more and more people were joining the queue. “Survival of the fittest.” He told himself as he continued to supply the never-ending eager hands.
A quarter of an hour later, Alan laughed aloud. “I know it’s impossible, but it’s happening. I don’t know how you do it, Joshua, but I’m glad you do.” He shouted down the line.

“I told you it wasn’t for us to decide who should eat and who should go hungry.” Joshua repeated his words.
Mike started to laugh as well, a hysterical kind of laugh erupted as he realised what Alan was saying. He hadn’t noticed before, too busy in his work. Now, now, he could see. It was impossible, but the containers were still half-full. It didn’t matter how much food you took out, the containers never emptied. Impossible but happening, like magic. A miracle, mass hysteria, the logic of his brain tried to tell him. No, that was impossible, you couldn’t make starving people believe they were eating and enjoying.
He began to cry, his tears mingling with his laughter. Miracle! He looked at Joshua - Messiah - the word popped into his head; it said everything.
A little later Dr. Evans and others joined them, too shocked to say anything.
“Dr Evans, can you arrange for someone to take over here, there is so much work to be done.” Joshua greeted them.
There was no shortage of relief workers, eager to take over the distribution.
Joshua led the way across the land, Alan, Mike and the news crew followed. Stopping, he turned to the doctor. ”You should have your people dig a well here.”
“But…” was the only word the doctor could say before Joshua went on.
“Can you not feel the water beneath your feet, Doctor?”
Doctor Evans looked down at his feet and suddenly jumped back, as water bubbled through the hard-crusted surface. They left him to organize things.
Joshua took hold of Julia Frazer’s arm. “Now, doctor, if you will take me to the sick children, I’ll see if there is anything I can do for them.”
Mike followed Joshua around in silence, feeling nothing, his emotions having long dried up, being replaced by an overwhelming sense of peace.
His news-team followed also, filming all the time without emotion, untouched by the miracles or the magic of the man, only knowing that this was stuff awards were made of.

Later in the evening, when Joshua had finished healing the children and had gone walking in the wasteland next to the camp, the news-team spoke to Mike.
"You're a canny bastard, Mike; you can sniff out a story before it happens. So when are you going to do the in-depth interview with Joshua?" Kevin greeted Mike.
"What interview?" He looked at them in disbelief. "Don't you realise what's been happening here today?"
"Yes, of course we do, we've been filming his every move."
"And you don't know who he is?"
"Exactly," Joe enthused. "That is what makes him such a good story. Mike, we'll be able to sell this world wide, and you seem to have built up a rapport with him, you'll be able to talk him into letting us travel with him so that we can film his work. We'll be famous, Mike."
"Go to hell, Joe." Mike stormed. He couldn't understand his friend's reaction, shit, what would it take to touch these people.
"Come on, Mike, the world has a right to know what he is doing. What are you saying, that you're not going to do the interview? You don't think the boss will accept that, do you, he'll just get someone else to do it and sack you." Kevin tried to talk some sense into him.
"Let him" Mike was going to say, I quit but instead he said. "I resigned this morning, I just hadn't realised it." He left them to it.
He would like to travel around with Joshua, if he was asked, not for the story, but for the honour of being allowed to witness Joshua's work.
As the early morning sun rose in the sky, the next morning, so did lush green healthy shoots of vegetables push their way up to the sun, eager to grow in this barren wasteland where Joshua had walked.
The land had been blessed.

Chapter Nine

Gemma woke with a start. She lay without movement, relieved to find it had only been a dream, nightmare. She cursed herself, what was she doing allowing nightmares to affect her so? She wiped the sweat from her face with a shaking hand. Perhaps they made everyone feel this way; she would have to ask Tad about it. She turned to him; he was still sleeping soundly, so she obviously hadn't screamed loud enough.

She had never dreamed before this last week. She knew that everyone was supposed to dream every night, but she never had. Even as a child in the orphanage, other children would wake up crying in the night, saying they had had a bad dream, she had never understood what they had meant.

She understood daydreaming and the feeling you got first thing in the morning. When you woke up but still feeling too comfy, too cosseted by the nights sleep that you didn't want to lose the feeling to the day, so you closed your eyes again and though nice thought, but that was all they were, thoughts, controlled conscious imaginings, not dreams.

If she did have dreams, as people insisted she must have, then they were things of the night, which never peeked into her conscious mind. There was nothing to ever flash in her mind, in the morning, from a strange memory that never existed. As far as she was concerned, her mind switched off a short while after she closed her eyes and only switched on again in the morning, or due to some disturbance in the night. But this past week she had dreams every night, they weren't nice and they were getting increasingly worst. She would be able to ignore the dreams if it wasn't for the effect they had on her the following day. The foreboding she felt, as if she was waiting for her dream to become reality. The lack of energy and enthusiasm, she felt as if her life force was being sucked dry. If this was what dreams were made of, well you could keep them.

She looked at the clock , 5a.m. she couldn't lay there any longer , sleep had been chased too far away. She slipped gently from the bed, not wanting to disturb Thadius, pulled on her dressing gown and crept downstairs. She made herself a cup of tea then went into the sitting room, drew back the curtains to admit the early morning sun.

The sun was already warm, so she unlocked the door and walked into the garden.
The early morning dew dampened and chilled her feet as she made her way to the bench.
She sat sipping her tea, relishing the quiet of the morning, the occasional bird-song and the sound of waves crashing on to the shore added to the serenity, allowing the warmth of the sun to chase away the blackness, that was left from the nightmare, from her soul. She was a fool, she knew, to allow a dream to take over her waking life, but she couldn't help it. She couldn't rid herself of the feeling that something bad was going to happen, anyway was it a normal dream. Was it normal to dream of a complete stranger for days and then have that strangers face appear on the television and in the newspapers. To have the world tell you that your nightmare, was a miracle worker, a messiah. The man in her dreams was Joshua; there was no doubt in her mind about that. He had the same leering smile, but in her dreams, he was far from being a saint, evil was more the mark. At first in her dreams, he had done nothing actually wrong, there was just a threatening sensation about him, but over the last few nights her dreams had become violent, Joshua had caused the violence. Last night had been the worse. She shivered at the memory of it.
In her dreams last night, she was in a place crowded with hundreds, maybe thousands of people. They were all watching Joshua, staring at him with stupid grins on their faces, mesmerised at the sight of him, their eyes shone with love. Then there was a scream, a bloodcurdling scream of someone in agony. She scanned the hundred of unknown faces, searching for the mouth that was no longer grinning but grotesquely shaped by the chilling scream. Another scream joined in and then another and she saw what they were screaming about. A woman was burning, her eyes were filled with terror as she watched the flames spreading up her body. No one tried to put out the flames, the people around her just starred, their faces a mask of horror, mesmerised as they had earlier been by Joshua.
They didn't even try to move away from her, they just watched and listened. Listened to her blood boiling, watched the ever hungry flames devouring, shrivelling and blackening her skin, gorging on the unprotected flesh, and the stench, the stench was…Gemma took

a gulp of tea for she could still taste the stench at the back of her throat.
Then another person started burning, and another, no one moved, they just watched. A few emitted a scream, but no one tried to run away to escape, for they knew there was no escape. The fire came from within them, they couldn't run away from themselves so they waited.
She couldn't wait, she couldn't just watch, she had to do something. She looked around for someone to help her, help her do what? She didn't know, she only knew that she couldn't just watch.
Then she saw Joshua, he was watching her, his smile sickening, he was enjoying her horror, as if he had put on the show especially of her.
Then she heard or felt, what? She didn't know, but she looked down at her self, she was naked. Her eyes widened with shock, not at her nakedness but at the black lines that had appeared on her body. She watched fascinated as the lines snaked their way down from her shoulders over her breast, travelling down to her stomach. Her skin began to crack, wide open crevices of flesh opened along the lines, like fault line in an earthquake. She tried to hold her flesh together with her hands, but it was impossible. A bright light emitted from the cracks and she thought she was going to burn, scared she was…she screamed.
Thankfully, she woke.
It was so real that even now she had to look at herself, expecting to see the crack lines, only her soft white skin stared back at her.
"Crazy" she told herself, a shudder ran through her, maybe she was crazy.
Or just tired, sick and tired of Joshua, she thought. Everyone was talking about him. On Sunday the congregation had even interrupted the sermon Thadius was giving to ask him if Joshua was the son of God, as if he knew, yet they expected him to have all the answers, and when he didn't their attitude was almost aggressive, as if they thought he was holding back some great secret.
"Hey, did you make it in the pot?"
She turned to see Thadius standing in the doorway, in just his jeans. She smiled, shaking her head. "Sorry, in the cup." She held it up as though in evidence. She heard him tutt as he turned away.

He returned five minutes later with a pot of tea and cups, he laid the tray on the grass in front of her then returned to the house, this time bringing out a large cushion, which he propped up against the armrest of the bench. He sat with his back against the cushion, one leg went to the back of the bench, he pulled her towards him so that she sat between his legs, her back against his chest.
"So what are you doing out here?" he asked, his arms wrapped around her.
"Just listening to the sounds of the morning. You can even hear the sea if your quiet." She snuggled deeper into his warmth and sighed.
"Hm, it's peaceful." He agreed.
"I love listening to the tide breaking on the shore, it's like someone breathing, you can never feel lonely." She said dreamily.
"Gem?"
"Hm?"
"If you were unhappy, you'd tell me wouldn't you?"
She turned her face up to look at him. "What do you mean?" her brow creased.
"If you were unhappy, you'd tell me, give me a chance to put things right."
She sat up a little and turned her body to face him. He looked seriously at her, too seriously. "Tad, you would know if I was unhappy, don't you worry about that. You'd definitely know." She smiled "What makes you think I'm unhappy?"
"You've been different these last few days." He shrugged.
"In what way?" She got up, pored the tea and put the cups within their reach then resumed her position, wrapping his arms around her.
"In what way?" she asked again.
"I don't know…you're quiet, distant…brooding."
"Brooding?" she turned right around now the flat of her palms against his chest, her chin resting on her hands
He was glad to see her smiling, the amusement sparkling in her eyes.
"Yes brooding," he laughed "Remember when we were trying for a baby and it took a few months before we struck lucky. Well after the second month, I didn't need you to tell me that you weren't pregnant, I knew as soon as I walked through the door. It was as if that little spot of blood changed the whole atmosphere of the house, there was a brooding, as if you were blaming me for not doing my job properly."

“I never blamed you. I was just disappointed; I hadn’t expected it to take so long. I had planned it just right for the baby to be born in May, instead I ended up carrying them right through to the end of September. But I never blamed you.”
“I know,” he brushed her hair from her face. “but all the same, there was a brooding and it’s here again now.”
“I’m not, there’s nothing wrong, honestly.”
“Gemma, you’re a very forceful lady,” He placed a gentle finger to her lips to stem her argument. “I don’t mean wilful, if anything I some times think you’re a little too easy going, people take advantage of your good nature. No, what I’m talking about are your moods, your feeling, they are so strong they’re almost a physical thing, that oozes over other people. When you’re happy, it’s everywhere, you can feel it in the house. At the moment you’re not happy, there’s a brooding.”
“I’m not unhappy, Tad,” she kissed him “and it has nothing to do you or anything you’ve done.”
“So there is something. Tell me, I want to know, I don’t like waking up every morning to find myself alone in the bed.”
“You’ll probably think I’m stupid.” He waited in silence so she went on. “It’s these dreams I’m having, they leave me feeling funny, as if I’m waiting for something bad to happen.”
“Are you serious? They’re only dreams, Gemma, you shouldn’t let them upset you.”
“Yes, I know I’m probably being daft, but…well, why do you think they’re such bad dreams, Tad. I mean it’s not normal to only have nightmares, is it?”
After a little thought, he said. “No, but then you’ve never been conscious of your dreams, perhaps you only aware of these, because they are bad. You’re not worrying about anything, are you?”
“Only my dreams” she laughed. “But, well, why are they always about Joshua? There’s something wrong about him, Tad, I don’t like him, he frightens me.”
“Frightens you, but why? He only does good.”
“I don’t know, but he does.” She had no real reason apart from her dreams and instinct.
“But he’s…”
“Don’t lets talk about him, Tad I’m tired of thinking about him, it’s like he’s haunting me.”

“Okay.” He kissed her “Just as long it’s nothing I’m doing.”
“Well you and Ben could find something else to talk about, other than Joshua”
“If it will stop you from brooding.” He agreed.
“I’m not brooding.” She picked up his cup and passed it to him.
“Just ignore me if I seem in a funny mood.” She advised him.
“Now that is an impossibility.” He sipped his tea. “Why don’t you give Rita a call.” He suggested. “Go out for the day, go shopping, have some lunch, spend some money that usually cheers you up.”
“But what about the kids, you’ve got to go over to Mrs Brown at Lifton’s.”
“That’s fine, I’ll drop the kids off, go straight over to see Mrs Brown. I should be back in time to pick Laura and Luke up from play school, and if I’m running late Ben will always pick them up.”
“Yeah, I’ll see if Rita’s free, are you sure.”
“Yes, besides I’ve got to keep my lady happy.” He put on his voice of martyrdom.
“Too true you have, mister.” She snuggled deeper into his arms.

Chapter Ten

“Bastard!” Marty Freeman swore, as he trudged down Lowestoft high street, his hands clenched in tight ball shaped fists dug deep into his jeans pockets, his arms and shoulders still twitched from the need to smash Maddog’s face in.
”I would have done for him an all, if it hadn’t been for his fucking devil dog.” He told himself. Then he gave a shiver as he remembered the snarling teeth of Gripper. That dog wanted to taste his blood even before he started threatening Maddog.
All your drug dealers had dogs now, staffies, Dobermans, Pit bulls, all the sorts of dogs that would rip your throat out just for the fun of it and still want their diner afterwards.
Marty hated all dogs, more, he believed that they hated him. Even the most docile of dogs hated him. He’d seen dogs in the park, stupid things, that had trouble keeping themselves on their feet where their tails waged so ferociously, more eager to lick the face of the child throwing the ball, than chasing the ball. Then they would spot him coming and he’d see their stance change, their muscles would tense, ready to attack at the slightest provocation. He could almost see the hairs on the dogs back rise one by one as he walked passed, their eyes boring into him, ignoring, for once, the calls of the children, until Marty was far enough away.
His mate Charlie, who was soft on dogs, reckoned it was because the dogs knew he was afraid of them, that they could smell his fear. Marty didn’t believe a word of it. The dogs just had enough sense, albeit instinct rather than intelligence, to recognise a real enemy, knowing that if he had his way, he’d string up every dog and gut them. They were nothing but parasites.
That’s what he would do to Gripper, if he ever got the chance. Come to think of it, that’s what he’d like to do to Maddog, right now.
“Bastard.” He swore aloud. It wasn’t as if it was the first time he’d asked for a fix without having the money for it, he’d always seen him right the next day.
But not tonight, no the sadistic bastard just kept repeating the same words over and over again. “No cash no stash.” Even when Marty had said he’d double the price the next day. When Marty had tried threatening, Maddog hadn’t said a word, he just gave Gripper his

head, only pulling him back just in time to stop him chewing on Marty's testicles. Shit, he'd almost pissed himself there and then. "Sorry about that, Marty." Maddog had smiled. "He's a bit too strong for me to hold sometimes, especially when he hasn't eaten. No hard feelings, hey Marty, come back when you got the cash." Marty had felt quite relieved when Maddog slammed the door shut between him and ten stones of muscle that was desperate for his throat.

Now he had to find some money quick, before his need turned him into a shaking useless wreck. He could break in some where, nick the laptop, ipad and any jewellery he could find. No, Jake would only need one look at him to know he was desperate for money and he'd stitch him up, knowing he'd accept anything he offered. He needed cash. Mugging? No, it was too much trouble, you never knew if they had any money on them or how they would react to the shock of being attacked. Some almost threw their money at you, begging you not hurt then, others would rather kill you, than hand over what was theirs, whether they had anything on them or not. No, it was too risky, you just couldn't tell with people. He'd leave that as the last resort.

The annoying thing was that in a few weeks time, money would be no problem, not once the holiday season started. There were enough caravan sites in Pakefiield, Kesingland and Lowestoft to keep him happy. Most of the caravans were left empty in the evenings, where the occupants were out getting pissed in the clubs and of course they always left the bulk of their money with their belongings, not wanting to carry all their holiday money with them in fear of losing it.

Most of the sites only had two or three security guards on duty at any one time. One was always on gate duty, to stop non-campers from coming on site to use the clubs without paying a visitors fee, which they pocketed half for themselves. Another guard spent most of the evening escorting the cashier around the bars, restaurant and café retrieving the cash from the tills, not wanting there to be too much temptation for the underpaid staff. Which left one guard to patrol the site, that's when he wasn't in the gatehouse with the other guard, drinking tea and having a chat, knowing they were only there for show, not being paid enough for any real vigilance.

Most of the sites could be reached from the beach or by walking along the cliff, so that you didn't even have to see a security guard, unless you were really stupid.
The real easy pickings came from the Theme Park, now that was a godsend, the place being packed with jostling crowds of people all excited at the prospect of having the shit frightened out of them, especially the teenagers. They were warned on their entry tickets to keep their money and belongings secure, but most of them took little notice of the warning, being too busy thinking about the thrill and shock they would get from hanging upside down, travelling at high speed in a corkscrew motion.
Marty looked upon it as him giving them a shock that they hadn't paid for nor expected, when they tried to get something to eat and found that they didn't have any money. Once he hadn't even had to nick anything, he'd found a bulging wallet under a seat of a ride he was on. He smiled to himself in anticipation of the happy days to come.
But what about tonight? He reminded himself. He would have to do something soon, he could feel the sweat starting to bead his face and back, sending shivers through him as a reminder that he needed his only love in his arm. He scratched unconsciously at the track marks on his arm.
Charlie called him a stupid cunt for injecting. He said he knew of a bloke who kept his pickled penis in a jar on the shelf, the bloke had started injecting into his prick because it was the only vein he had left to use, as all the others had collapsed. His prick went gangrene and he had to have amputated. The bloke kept it on the shelf as a deterrent, for when he got the urge to go back to drugs.
Marty told him it was a load of old crap, it was just one of those stories that go around, the ones that everybody hears about but nobody knows where it came from.
Still he noticed that his thighs had move in closer to each other, at the memory of the story, as if to protect his unhappy member.
"Don't worry, we like the girlies too much for anything like that." He told his shrinking penis, as though it were a being in it's own right, he gave it a little squeeze with his hand for reassurance.
He stopped suddenly in his tracks. Of course, Mrs Chambers, the name popped into his head. He had done her place once before. A

rich old biddy in her seventies, who lived all alone in a big old house.
Before he had gone there out of desperation, not really expecting to be able to get near the place for security systems, but to his amazement, there hadn't been any, not even an alarm on the windows and doors.
It had been one of the easiest jobs he had ever done, and the silly old cow left an awful lot of money around the house, where even a three year old could find it. He remembered how at the time, he had expected the lights to be switched on and to find half the Suffolk Constabulary to be there saying "Surprise." It had been that bloody easy. He didn't even have to worry about her waking up and finding him, for her snoring echoed around the whole bloody house.
He was still laughing the next day, but he had soon stopped. Mrs. Chambers was not only rich but influential, and it seemed that every officer in the force wanted to nick the man responsible.
Marty had only taken money so there was no need for him to worry about anything being traced back to him, but the law made a nuisance of itself, it was everywhere.
Strange, Marty mused, you could beat up some old bloke, nick his pension, which might be all the money that the poor old sod has, so that he as to go and beg money from the ss, just so that he can eat, and he'll be lucky if he gets a copper to call on him for five minute. Yet nick a few hundred from someone who is loaded, the money being no more than loss change to them, and the law comes out with all the vengeance of someone looking for a child molester. That was the power of money he supposed, or at least the power of a lot of money.
"Still, I'm no snob." He told himself, money was money and he didn't care who it belonged to, as long as it became his.
Yeah, he'd give Mrs Chambers a go. Of course, she'd probably had a security system put in by now but he'd still have a look. From what he knew about Mrs. Chambers, it was possible that she hadn't fitted any alarms, instead decided to keep a gun by her bed in the hope that someone might try to burgle her again and this time she'd be able to have the satisfaction of getting her pound of flesh. She was a ferocious old girl, even her snoring had an assertiveness to it.
He came to the street where her house stood. His footstep became silent, his pace remained leisurely, the only difference now being

that he kept to the shadow where possible, which was most of the way as the street wasn't well lit and the houses were all laid well back from the road, so he didn't have to worry about the light from them.
He reached Mrs Chambers house and stole his way quietly up the drive then made his way to the back of the house. He froze as he turned the corner and saw light streaming from the back room windows. He stepped back into the shadows, shit, he'd have to wait for her to go to bed, but that could take hours and he needed his fix now. Perhaps if she was watching television he could get in and out without her even noticing. He would have to try, his arms were beginning to hurt rather than itch and soon his stomach would begin to cramp. He decided to go for it, even if she did hear him, she was an old lady, he'd have no problem putting her down.
He'd just have to check that she was alone, it would be no good if she had company. He kept to the wall as he edged his way around. The back door was wide open, she must be in the garden. Sweat washed over his body, as he expected to feel the cold steel of a shotgun pushed into the back of his neck. He turned and released his breathe when he realise no one was behind him.
She must be out here, he reasoned, why else would the back door be open? Unless…unless she'd got herself a fucking dog. He scanned the garden for movement.
Then he saw her, she was kneeling in the middle of the garden. Marty almost laughed out loud, she couldn't be gardening, it was pitch dark out here, unless she was senile? As he moved closer to her he could see that her hands were held motionless in front of her, her head was tilted up to the sky.
"What the hell…" he said as he followed her gaze. "OH SHIT!" he fell to his knees.

Chapter Eleven

Jim Harding walked along the cliff top towards Kessingland. He had finished his work a couple of day ago but had decided to stay on for another week, at his uncles request. He liked his uncle, to his surprise, and thought it was time they got to know each other a bit better. They had met a couple of times before when Jim was still a boy, but he had always been uneasy in his uncles company. He realised now that it was due to his mother's behaviour rather than his uncle's.

She always had the whole family one edge with all her do's and don'ts in front of their uncle, that they regarded him, unjustly it seemed, as some sort of an ogre.

Ben and he had discussed it the other night and they both had a good laugh. Ben had always thought his four nephews rather strange, they never seemed to go out, and yet they appeared to have no indoor interests. They never seemed to talk, laugh or fight between themselves. In truth Ben had felt uncomfortable in their company, especially after being used to the rough and tumble of the children at the orphanage.

Jim told him how his mother started to threaten them about their behaviour as soon

as she received his letter saying that he'd be visiting. They had all dreaded his visit as they weren't allowed to go out and play, in fact they were too scared to do anything, while he was around in case their mother had a heart attack, she used to get herself so uptight.

"Strange" Ben had said, "She was always so relaxed as a young girl."

"She still is, there's no way you can shock my mother and I had tried really hard when I was younger, she always took everything in her stride. But as soon as she knew you were visiting she changed, so we naturally thought it was your fault. The sad thing about it is that she never enjoyed your visits because she worried herself sick about it, poor old mum." Jim had told his uncle he also confessed that he had always been a bit afraid of clergymen after that, until he started to associate with them through his work and found them to be quite human. He had decided it must have been his uncle who was an old misery.

Now he was enjoying becoming acquainted with the man rather than the ogre. He also liked the area. It was quiet and the natives were friendly, if somewhat nosey when it came to strangers. He found that by telling them he was visiting his uncle, Ben Mason, that they warmed to him immediately, it was their reaction to his uncle that made him wonder about the man. It pleased him to realise that his uncle was such a popular man.
He found that staying at his uncle's cottage had a calming effect on him, even now as they were in the middle of decorating his sitting room, there was still a tranquillity about the place. Besides there was nothing for him to rush home for, no one special waiting for him, not since Pat had left him eight months ago. Eight months and it still hurts him to think of her. "Bloody fool" he reprimanded himself.
It had come as such a shock, he hadn't even realised that she was unhappy with their relationship, believing that she felt the same about him as he felt about her. He had thought that they would be together forever. At first when she had told him she was leaving, that she was moving in with Paul, he hadn't believed her, thinking it was some sort of sick joke. But as he watched her pack, he realised that nothing he said could thaw the coldness she felt towards him, he had got angry, so angry that he had scared her, he had scared himself as well for he realised that he wanted to hit her. He left and didn't return to the flat for a week. The flat felt so empty, even now after all this time. He missed the closeness of being in the easy company of someone special.
H realised that he had stopped and was staring out at sea. Lights flashed on the horizon and he wondered if the storm would roll inland. There was nothing quite like watching a raging storm at sea from the safety of the shore for calming the soul, or perhaps it was the hour's walk and the two pints of bitter at the pub, that made him feel so peaceful.
The clouds were moving quickly through the sky and he wondered how long it would be before the storm would strike the shore. He was only about ten minutes walk away from Ben's cottage so he lingered, enjoying the sight of the changing sky. Being a Londoner he never really watched the sky, unless there were threatening black clouds, now he was enjoying the beauty of the sight.

The sky began to clear, which surprised him, and he felt a tinge of disappointment that the storm wasn't going to join him. He was about to go on his way, when a coloured light appeared in the sky. Not quite a light, but a shimmering of green, yellow, red and black wavered through the air. He watched fascinated, as the illuminations shimmered and danced in the sky. Slowly the erratic wavering began to slow, to settle forming a shape.
He tried to work out the picture that the lights were trying to form. Suddenly the whole thing started to explode like the finale of a firework exhibition, only silent, which gave it a quality of eeriness. Light fused and flashed as they merged together. It stopped suddenly, and Joshua's face lit up the sky.
"Oh, my dear god." Jim mumbled. It wasn't possible, but it was, he could even hear Joshua speaking. Joshua had turned the sky into a bloody great television screen to give his sermon.
Jim started running. He had to tell Ben, he would never forgive him, if he allowed him to miss this.
He made it to Ben's cottage in four minutes flat.

Chapter Twelve

Lewis Dowell sniggered, a wide grin filled his face as he climbed down from the chair, that he'd been standing on so that he could see out of his cell window. "Won't be able to get me now." He hissed another snigger. "Did you hear what he said?" He asked the shadows that he knew were there, even if he couldn't see them at this precise moment, they were always there, waiting, taunting.
A chuckle escaped him, his hand shot to his mouth as he tried to stifle the sound. He mustn't make too much noise, else they'd find out what he was intending to do and stop him. Still he chuckled to himself, he couldn't help it, he felt so good.
All those years they had waited, every night terrorising his mind, filling it with the horrors that awaited him when he joined them. But now he wouldn't be joining them. He was escaping, Joshua had said he could.
"Did you hear him, Margaret, hey, did you hear him? Poor, poor, Margaret, so long you've waited, only to be cheated." His mocking was no more than a whisper.
Margaret had been the first, initially he hadn't noticed her, if he had, well perhaps things would have been different, but then again they probably wouldn't have. He chuckled.
In fact he had noticed her, he just hadn't realised it at the time. She was such a small thing, just a slight movement that he had sometimes caught out of the corner of his eye, but when he looked there was nothing to be seen.
Margaret wasn't silly, she knew she only had to wait, that there would be others, she could afford to be patient. He had seen to it that she didn't have to wait too long for Carol to join her. Together they united their strength, knowing that time and he would give them power, so they waited.
Within two years there was ten of them and he was no longer able to ignore them. He could see them as a collective shadow, could hear their whispers. He had enjoyed seeing and hearing them at first, for he knew they were still in his power, that he still controlled them even though they were dead, and that had excited him even more. He didn't need sex, that was just part of the parcel, it was the control that gave him his high. The power he had over them, to be able to do

what ever he wanted, to experiment, to play and all the time they had pleaded, begged, made promises that they both knew they would never be able to keep.
Like a fool, he had enjoyed seeing them believing that he had control over them in death just as he had in life, for the three or four days he had them in his power before murdering them. Some he hadn't even murdered, they had died while he played with them.
He realised his mistake by the time there were twenty of them. He had no control over them now. Their constant chattering forever filled his ears and mind. It got to a point where he couldn't sleep for their voices in his head, haunting him day and night. His world was in constant darkness as their shadows surrounded him. He no longer had the power to still their voices, to make their shadows diminish from his eyes.
It was their fault that he had gone for the child, he wasn't really interested in children, but he needed the feeling of being in control. He was weakened by the lack of sleep, because of their constant nagging. He couldn't even remember the last time he had eaten, being too tired to think of food, besides he had no hunger for food. Only the hunger for power and control gnawed away at him.
He had gone out in search for a woman, to staunch his hunger pangs, but as he walked around looking he began to doubt his strength. He knew he needed a lot of strength as some of these women put up one hell of a fight, so he had decided on a girl child.
It had been easy, he had no trouble controlling her small struggles, with his hand clamped tightly around her mouth he headed for his car, the boot was open and waiting a couple of yards ahead.
Suddenly his ladies were there, massed into a dense, deep darkness, blinding him with their shadows. Their screams of revenge filled his mind, no longer a choir of whispers but individual screams of accusations, vengeful plots of what they would do to him.
"No! you can't leave the house, you're bound there by my power." He had screamed at them.
They only laughed at him, some sniggered. He tried to see passed their shadows, he knew his car was only a little way ahead of him, if he could reach the car he could get away from them.
"Yes, drive, get away." The voices urged.

Why would they want him to escape? Was it escape or was it a trap? He couldn't think, the voices were screaming in his mind, confusing his thoughts. He needed to clear his mind, to think.
He stood motionless, still his arm gripped the child tightly but his hand had slipped from her mouth, allowing her to scream. A scream that didn't reach his brain but was heard by others in the street.
The child's mother's screams joined her daughter's. Two men who were painting the outside window frames of a house further down the road rushed to the mother's assistance, as she fought to release her child from his grip.
A neighbour who realised what was happening phoned the police before joining the mother as she rushed her daughter into the safety of their home.
The first Dowell knew of what was happening was when he felt something like a iron bar strike his chin, he went down and suddenly he could see again, the shadow and the voices had disappeared, leaving only the sight of two angry men standing over him. One rubbed the knuckles of his right hand, rage flared in his eyes.
"Fucking pervert, needs castrating." He said to his companion and gave Dowel a well aimed kick with his heavy steel capped boot.
Pain had seared through him like a red-hot poker, every nerve in his body screamed out, sending bile from his stomach to choke in his throat. His muscles contracted, bringing his body into the shape of a ball, his hand automatically went to his testicles in an effort to stem the pain. His mind travelled with the pain, making his body almost oblivious to the kicks the two men were hailing down on him. Each kick helped him on his journey to the soft blackness of unconsciousness.
He had no memory of the police, their questions, the trial that followed the discovery of his ladies bodies. His mind was too confused, still not being able to understand how the shadows had got out of the house.
He had been in Broadmoor for fifteen years now and every night of those years, his ladies had visited him. Taunting him with the tortures that awaited him when he joined them in death.
His ladies over the years had become very imaginative and told him of the many ways in which they would tear his soul apart, promising they would put him back together again so that they could start their new game. All those years they had torn apart his mind with their

vengeance, making him live in terror of dying, knowing for him death held no escape, only capture and an eternity of pain and suffering.
"Until tonight." He laughed out loud.
He removed some wire from his bedstead. He sniggered the joy that bubbled uncontrollably from deep within him, as he patiently straightened the bends from the wire. He wished his ladies were here to see his escape but they hadn't appeared tonight. They must have heard what Joshua had said and were sulking somewhere.
He had been pacing the floor of his cell, waiting for their shadows to arrive when he saw Joshua appear in the sky. It was as if everything around him had diminished as he climbed onto the chair to get a better view of Joshua through the window
For the first time in his life he had felt an inner peace as he listened to the man talk of his father's love, and when Joshua said that his father welcomed everyone into his kingdom, especially the sinners, Dowell had known what he had to do.
There was no time to lose, he had to do it now before some do-gooder got Joshua to change his mind.
He tied one end of the now straightened wire into a noose, and then tied the other end onto the window.
"Goodbyes, my lovelies, sorry I won't be able to join you, but I go to a better place." he said to the shadows that were no longer there. He slipped the noose around his neck then kicked away the chair beneath his feet.
He didn't struggle as the wire bit into his neck, for he welcomed death now that it no longer held any terror.
The shadows rushed to him, only now he could see their individual faces smiling at him.
"No." he screamed in his mind, as he felt their hands touching him. His fingers clawed at his throat as he realised his mistake, but the wire had cut too deep for him to pull it away.
His ladies pulled down on his feet, almost decapitating him. Lewis Dowell was now theirs.

Chapter Thirteen

Joshua was seen by the world that night and was heard in every language of every country. People of every religion claimed Joshua as their God's true messiah, even people who had no initial religious beliefs changed their mind or found themselves touched by his words. To everyone Joshua was a hero who had come to save the people and perhaps the world. To everyone, that is except Gemma, or so it felt to her.

Of course, scientist didn't believe he was a messiah, which they wouldn't considering they had spent their lives believing in Evolution, abandoning all thoughts of a God long ago. The scientists denial of Joshua, did nothing to comfort Gemma, if anything it made her doubt her own feelings more, being unsettled by the fact that she found herself in agreement with them for the first time. But even the scientists couldn't make her change her mind about Joshua, so the next morning she found herself feeling alienated among everyone she knew.

Worrying about Joshua's effect on the world, only helped to fan her rage when she had to listen to Mrs Chambers stupidity, not that it needed much help when it came to dealing with her. By the time she reached home she found herself unable to control her anger.

"Evil old witch." She ranted as she slammed the car keys onto the table, not even bothering to say hello to Ben and Jim who had arrived while she was out, eager to talk to Thadius about the night before.

"Gemma, what's wrong?" Thadius asked.

"Bloody Mrs Chambers, that's what's wrong. "Evil old bitch."

Thadius winced at her swearing, not appreciating her language but having long ago excepted it as part of her when really angry "Wow, Gemma, calm down, what did she do this time?" Thadius tried to soothe her.

"Well, you know I had to go around there to pick up the stuff for the fete this morning, because it was the only time convenient for her, as if she's the only one with things to do, so I obeyed her orders and turned up at the arranged time and she asks what I want. I told her and she said that the fete wouldn't be necessary now as no one

needed the church now that Joshua was here. Pompous old cow." Gemma said
Thadius laughed. "That's it, that's what made you so angry?" His eyebrows rose, knowing there must be more.
Gemma looked away from his gaze. "And you'll never guess who she has staying with her as a house guest, Marty Freeman, can you believe that? It seems they both saw the light together." The sneer in her voice made her feelings clear.
"I take you didn't see Joshua last night, if you had you might be able to understand her compassion towards Marty." Ben said. He had always been touched by compassion but felt more hopeful for a world at peace after last night.
Gemma had, seen Joshua, because Thadius wanted her to be with him. But turned away as soon as he started talking, you had to look at him to hear his lies.
"Oh I saw her compassion, her eyes shone and a smile of pure joy was on her face as she spewed her dirty thoughts from her evil mouth. She calls herself a Christian. Bloody hypocrite."
"See I knew it." Thadius sounded quite pleased with himself. "What did she say?"
"Nothing" she answered too fast.
"Gem, defender of the faith, you aren't. Protector of the family, well that is something different." He knew Gemma wouldn't have been that angry over something that silly. Mrs Chambers must have said something detrimental about them, and not for the first time, for Gemma to be so angry. "What did she say?"
"Oh, just the usual stuff." Gemma lied. "You know, how you should never been able to keep you job when you married me, me being a foundling and all."
"You're joking?" Jim said a little shocked. He found it hard to believe that people still used that word. "What's that got to do with Thadius's job?"
"No, Mrs Chambers tried to have Thadius thrown out of the parish as soon as she heard they were getting married. She said it was a vicar's responsibility to marry someone decent with a good background." Ben told his nephew. "Of course she has had to accept Gemma over the years, but she hasn't liked it, women like her don't take defeat happily."

“I need a cup of tea.” Gemma excused herself. She needed to release her rage but knew it wouldn’t be welcome in front of Ben and Jim, which made it harder to contain, she’d have to be content with slamming the cupboard doors as she made the tea. She hadn’t been aware of Thadius following her from the room and gave a start when she heard his voice behind her.
“What did she say, Gem?” Thadius asked as he closed the kitchen door behind him. “I’ve told you, she...”
“No.” he interrupted her. “She been saying that sort of thing for over seven year and you’ve always laughed it off.” He took her hand and sat her down at the table, he sat down facing her. “Gemma, tell me. I know what you’re like, you’ll let it eat away at you until you explode and you’ll say something to her without any justification and then you will feel guilty about it.”
“Oh, I’ve got plenty of justification.” Gemma said.
“Come on babe, tell me.”
Gemma let out a long sigh, as she studied his face, deciding whether or not to tell him.
“So it was about me.” Thadius said knowingly.
“You know what she’s like if she can’t control someone with her ideas, that person automatically becomes beyond contempt. Someone really should tell her..”
“Did you say anything?” Thadius asked. Gemma was a volatile person and he never knew quite what to expect.
“No. I felt like slapping her around a bit, and if we had been standing at the top of some stairs, well.” Her eyes flashed her sentiment “but no, I didn’t say anything. You don’t need defending, your work holds it’s own merit and if she can’t appreciate the care you give, well.”
Thadius smiled as he imagined the scene. Gemma standing erect as the woman spoke, her arms crossed beneath her breast, her hands gripping tightly on to her jumper in an effort to stop them tearing at the eyes of the woman, who’s words stabbed so deep. Her head raised a little to high, her chin jutting out as if tempting a fist, so that she could rent to the rage that was building. Her lips pouting, her cheeks tinged pink and her eyes prickling with tears that she kept at bay without a flicker of a blink. The eyes staring, a look that would frizzle up the words, if not the soul of any half intelligent human being. Then with a blink Mrs Chambers would have known that she

had been dismissed as a waste of space. Gemma would turn away and walk determinedly to the car, a slight tremor of her hand as she fitted the key into the lock would be the only sign of the effect the woman's words had on her.
He laughed aloud, at the image.
Gemma looked up at him with surprised eyes. "What?"
"Nothing." Shook his head and then leaned forward and kissed her lip. "Thanks, for not saying anything. I know it must have been hard."
"Thanks, but I'm not sure I did the right thing, Tad. If someone told her what every one thought about her, perhaps she'd learn to keep her mouth shut. Evil old…"
"That's it, you concentrate on the old bit, and try to forget the bat bit. Besides one flash from those eyes of yours and she'd know she was heading straight to purgatory." He gave her a knowing wink.
"Well," she felt a little embarrassed now by her anger. "Anyway you're wrong. She so thick skinned that it would take a sledgehammer to get through to her. A million year old fossil would have more sensitivity than her. And to think I was concerned about her because she had taken Marty into her home, it's him we ought to be worried for."
"Gemma, please, I don't understand why you've let her upset you so much. I know she says things that we all find hard to forgive but…"
"Yes, well I sometimes think that too much forgiveness breeds abuse." she bristled.
Thadius held up his hands in mock surrender. "I'm the good guy, remember."
"I know I'm sorry. I'll make the tea, and forget all about her. What's Ben and Jim doing here?" she asked.
"Oh, Ben wanted to discuss Joshua, after last night's appearance." He tried to make his words light, knowing that last nights show did nothing to change her feelings towards Joshua. He didn't understand her fears, even though they had talked about it last night. But he respected her feelings. He helped her make the tea then carried in the tray.
"I shouldn't worry about what Mrs Chambers said, Gemma." Ben greeted her return. "I think people will be flooding into the church, now that they've heard Joshua."

“Oh, please Ben.” The thought sickened her, why, she didn’t know, it wasn’t as if Ben had meant to slight Thadius in any way. No, it was something deeper than that.
“I think.” Thadius tried to explain Gemma’s outburst to Ben. “That you’ve just met your fist case of Joshua phobia.”
“What.” Ben Stammered. ”You saw Joshua and you weren’t touched by his reverence, by his love?” He saw the child he had always loved as his own in a new and confusing light. “But, Gemma, he’s our saviour.”
“Some, saviour. I was listening to the radio earlier, it said that over four hundred murderers committed suicide last night in their cells after seeing Joshua…”
“But you can’t blame Joshua for that.” Ben interrupted; the contempt in her voice frightened him. “Those people were crazy, they had to be otherwise they would never have committed murder in the first place. You can’t hold Joshua responsible.”
“Some of them left notes, Ben, saying Joshua told them to do it. He doesn’t sound like a saviour to me.”
“I can assure you he told no one to harm themselves. I listened to him and he only spoke of love. Didn’t you even listen to him.” He accused, as he felt his anger towards her rising for the first and he didn’t like himself for it.
“No, I didn’t, you had to look at his face to hear his words and I couldn’t do that. Maybe he said different things to different people, I don’t know, but don’t you think it strange that every religion has claimed him as their messiah. For the first time in history they all agree on something, all the different religions with their different gods and they all agree.” Gemma said. That more than anything set off alarm bells to her.
“I don’t think it strange at all, it just proves he is who he is. There is only one God, because we give him different names and have different understanding of his words
doesn’t mean that we have a different God. Surely you can understand that. Joshua confirmed it last night.”
Gemma opened her mouth to say something, but changed her mind. She didn’t want to hurt him by arguing, although she had a deep seated urge to try to change his mind about Joshua, she wasn’t prepared to put their love at risk. Instead she said. “I’m sorry, Ben, I would love to agree with you, but I can’t. Call it female intuition or

stupidity, what ever you like, but it's wrong, don't ask me why its wrong or how I know. I only know that Joshua doesn't feel right. I will leave you to chat, as I have a pile of ironing to do. I'll see you later." Gemma picked up her tea and left the room.
Ben went to follow her but Thadius held him back. "Leave her, Ben."
Ben's face looked grey. "But we can't leave her, we have to talk to her." Ben's hand shook as he took hold of Thadius's, pleading. "You heard her, Thadius, she hates him."
"Gemma doesn't hate him. Gemma couldn't hate anyone." Thadius tried to reassure the old man and Ben did look suddenly old.
"She has a right to her own opinion, Ben." said Jim. He also concerned by his uncle's appearance.
"You don't understand, Jim, she's turning her back on Joshua, turning her back on the lord. By her hate she's condemning her soul to everlasting damnation."
His uncles words shocked Jim, the conviction in his voice chilling. He looked to Thadius and was surprised to see that he wasn't completely unbelieving. Jim had never been a religious man finding blind faith a bit of an enigma, far beyond his understanding. Oh, he had been touched by Joshua last night but only in as much as an inspiring experience, not unlike the first time he had gone diving. Surprised at the new unexpected beauty, having his eyes opened to a new and exciting wonders confirming how little he knew or understood about everything. But no more than that, nothing like Ben's conviction, but now he understood his uncle's colour and physical aging. He was afraid for Gemma.
He heard Thadius speaking gently to Ben, his words strong and comforting and for the first time Jim saw him as many of his parishioners must know him.
"You're wrong, Ben. Don't worry God will see Gemma for who she is, not for her words, as he sees all of us, by our souls and he'll only find beauty in Gemma. You know that's the truth."
"How can he? She's spurning his son. He can't give her his heart if she won't accept it." Ben's eyes were staring wide and he wasn't listening to reason.
"We're his children, Ben, he won't expect too much from us too soon. He understands that we all make mistakes, that we all fall now

and then, it's what's in our hearts and souls that counts. Gemma is safe, you of all people must know that." Said Thadius.
"No! this is different, can't you feel it? This is the final calling, if you turn away from him now, you're lost forever. We've got to save her, Thadius, before it's too late."
Thadius was surprised by Ben's agitated state and wondered if this new revelation hadn't been too much for him. Ben wasn't the kind of man who talked of hellfire and damnation. He would have to handle things carefully for if he allowed Ben to talk to Gemma like this, it wouldn't do either of them any good. "I don't think now is a good time, Ben"
"But…" Ben started to say.
"Ben, Gemma's been under a lot of strain this past year. I don't think she'd be able to take this sort of confrontation right now." Thadius could see by Ben's face that
he'd struck the right chord, there was still concern in his eyes but he seemed less agitated.
"But I thought Laura was alright now." Ben said
"She is, but Gemma's been having nightmares lately. She wakes up in the night and rushes in to make sure Laura's alright. She say's she dreams that death has come for Laura." So he wasn't telling the complete story, Ben wouldn't understand if he did.
"Why now? While Laura was ill it was Gemma that kept everyone going." Said Ben.
"Probably because Laura is better, Gemma feels that she let go a little."
"Are you saying that she's heading for some sort of breakdown, because if you are, I think you should have told me." Ben was still concerned.
"No, Ben, I'm not saying that. It's like you said, Gemma was the one who was strong while we were all falling apart. Now that she doesn't have to worry anymore she's just letting out all her fears and anger. I think she deserves a little time and understanding to allow her to sort out her feelings, that's all." Thadius hadn't thought about it before but now that he had put it into words, perhaps it wasn't so far from the truth. Gemma had been acting a little strange lately, a bit more moody than usual.

"I didn't realise." Ben said. "Her outburst earlier wasn't like her, was it." His face still showed signs of worry but it looked more natural. "We did crack up a bit, when Laura was ill, didn't we."
"Natural reaction, we were all under a lot of strain." Thadius agreed.
"She'll be alright won't she. Do you think she ought to see a doctor? I mean…"
"No, she just needs time and tender loving care." Thadius said.
"I think I'll go and have a word with her." Ben said rising from the chair.
"You're not going to mention Joshua, are you?" Thadius panicked.
"No, I'm just going to say I'm sorry."

Later, when Ben and Jim had gone home, Thadius told Gemma what he had said.
"You told Ben I was having a nervous breakdown!" Gemma repeated his words in disbelief.
"I had no choice I had to say something, it was for Ben's benefit. He was acting really strange, he reckoned we had to save your soul because you were damning it to the hellfire's. I was expecting him to do an exorcism on you." Ben explained.
Gemma laughed, Ben had never thought like that. He was the sort of person who believed there was good in everyone, however bad their deeds. "And this was all because of what I said about Joshua? I don't believe it."
"It's true, you should have seen him. I thought he was going to have a stroke or something, his face turned grey. It was only when I said that perhaps, this was your reaction to Laura's illness, that he calmed down. Besides I'm not so sure there isn't a bit of truth in what I said."
"You what" Gemma said
"Well you are over reacting about Joshua a bit. You've never had any strong reaction to religious beliefs before so why do you hate Joshua so. What has he done that's so bad, apart from cure children who were suffering or dying, feed starving people and preached world love and understanding."
Gemma was silent for a while, then took a deep breathe and said "Put like that, he sounds more like an hero than an enemy."
"No one to be afraid of." Thadius agreed.
"So why do I feel the way I do, so full of dread?"

Thadius shrugged. “Perhaps you resent him for not being around when Laura was ill.” He suggested.
“That’s ridiculous.”
“No, Gem, think about it. What does anyone think when they have children. They expect to get a lot of joy from watching them grow, for them to marry, have children of their own. And one day for them to bury us. No one ever contemplates that they might have to bury that child at the age of three. We all know that it happens but it happens to some other poor soul, not us.” Thadius was silent for a moment. “I know that what ever life has in store for us, we will never have to suffer again the way we all suffered when Laura had Leukaemia. Nothing could ever be that bad again.”
Tears streamed down Gemma’s face. Thadius took her in his arms and held her tightly to him allowing her to cry as she had never cried before.

Chapter Fourteen

Marty sat on the bed staring at the hypodermic needle, which was filled and waiting on the bedside cabinet. Beads of sweat lined his brow. He tried to swallow the dryness from his throat. Slowly he pushed up the sleeve of his shirt then took a strip of rubber and tied it tightly around his upper arm, with a shaking hand he picked up the needle and aimed it at the protruding thick blue vein.

"No. I can't." He slapped the needle back onto the cabinet. He ran to the window, wanting to put some distance between himself and the thing he needed so much.

"God help me." He cried as he sank to his knees. "Give me Strength." He pleaded. He wanted to pray but didn't know how to. He looked up into the sky wishing he could see Joshua's face there, knowing he'd be safe under the gaze of his haloed eyes.

Why had he gone out this morning, he cursed. If he had stayed in, he wouldn't be feeling the way he was now. He hadn't even thought about drugs since he had knelt with Mrs Chambers in the garden, listening to Joshua as he spoke from the sky. Mrs Chambers had taken him in, saying that Joshua must have meant for them to be together.

He had done a few jobs around the place, which the old girl wasn't able to do, in repayment for her hospitality and surprisingly they got on really well together. Marty had never felt so good in all his life, this peace he felt was better than any high he had ever known.

Then this morning he had gone for a walk, feeling the need for some fresh air, having stayed in for the last few days. He wasn't going anywhere in particular, just walking, enjoying the sun on his face. He heard someone call his name and without thinking he stopped and turned to see Maddog, without Gripper, running to catch him up.

"Marty, where have you been? You didn't come back the other night." Maddog asked while trying to catch his breathe.

"The other night?" then Marty had remembered. "Oh, no I didn't need to."

"Hey come on, Marty, You're not gonna take offence because of what I said the other night, are you? I was only joking mate, there's no need to go to someone else. I've never let you down before have

I? I even went around your place looking for you, but you weren't there."
"I moved out." Marty said.
"Yeah, anywhere nice?"
"So-so." Marty didn't want the likes of him going around there, bothering Mrs Chambers. "Anyway, Maddog," It seemed strange calling him by that now, but he had never known him by any other name. "I don't use the stuff anymore, so I won't be needing your services now."
"What do you mean, you're not using it anymore?" Not Marty as well, Maddog thought. This was getting fucking ridiculous he'd already had six of his regulars saying the same thing. "Look, to show there's no hard feelings, here you are, half price." He pushed the drug into Marty's hand.
Marty wouldn't take it. "I don't need it. Joshua is the only stimulant I need, faith my only high."
Not fucking Joshua again, what did the bloke have against him. At this rate he'd be lucky if he could give the stuff away, Maddog grumbled to himself. Of course. "Look, Marty, take it." He put the drug into Marty's shirt pocket. "I know you don't want it, but take it, just in case the cravings get too bad. Even Joshua wouldn't expect you to go cold turkey." He patted Marty's pocket as a reminder that in was there. "Be lucky." He said and walked away. A smile spread across his face. It's no good being the proud owner of an unwanted commodity, he told himself. Let's see you resist now Marty, my son. So he'd have to give some of it away, as long as he could keep them using, they'd be back. He wasn't about to let his lucrative business go to pot.

As Marty walked home, he pondered on what Maddog had said about going cold turkey. It was strange but he hadn't had any cravings since seeing Joshua. It had been days since he had anything and he didn't have any withdrawal symptoms.
Or so he had thought, now as he knelt in front of the window praying for Joshua to appear, every nerve in his body could hear the needles call, every nerve screamed out for relief.
He turned to look at the needle and felt himself being torn apart, not knowing which way to go.
Rising to his feet, he cursed Maddog aloud.

Chapter Fifteen

Mrs Chambers had been correct in her prediction about people not needing the church now that they had Joshua. It was a half hour after Sunday service should have begun and the church was empty apart from Gemma, Thadius, the children, Ben and Jim. Mr Allen, the organist, had just left after Thadius told him it wasn't worth waiting any longer.
"I can't understand it. I would have thought people would have flocked in." Ben said for the fourth time as they stood in the church doorway.
"They have Joshua, they don't need the church anymore." Gemma told him, her voice heavy. "Why don't you and Jim go in doors and make your selves some tea. I'll just give Thadius a hand collecting up the hymn books."
"I've a better idea. I'll take the children home with me; you and Thadius can join us later for lunch." Ben gave a quick look towards Thadius who was already putting things away. "I think Thadius might want a bit of time to himself." He turned to the children. "Laura, Luke would you like to come to the park with me, and we'll see mummy and daddy at my house for lunch?" he asked. They were more than eager to go with their grandfather knowing that he would spoil them.
"You two be good of granddad." Gemma warned them as she kissed them goodbye.
"They always are." Ben said in their defence.
Gemma watched them leave before turning back to the church. Thadius was collecting the hymnbooks. "Bens taken the children to the park, we're joining him for lunch."
"That's nice of him." Thadius answered vaguely, his mind on other things.
"I'm sorry, babe." Gemma touched his arm to stop his movement.
"What? Oh this…" he gave her a quick smile.
Gemma sat in a pew. She preferred the church when it was empty of people. There was serenity about it, as if it was closed off from the outside world. She felt it's stillness wrap around her like a comfortable cocoon. Thadius sat beside her; he took her hand in his and rested it in his lap

"What will happen?" she asked.
"I don't know. The decision isn't ours, it never has been."
Gemma was surprised by his calm. "I thought you'd be upset or disappointed, but you're not."
Thadius thought for a moment then said "I'm surprised. I, like Ben, expected the congregation to grow." He gave a shrug of his shoulders. "I don't presume to understand what is going on. Perhaps it's his way of telling us that we've been doing things wrong. I don't know but I'm willing to accept his guidance. I believe he'll show us the way we must go, that's good enough for me."
"But people will still need you for weddings, christenings and the likes."
"I hope they'll need me for a lot more than that. We'll have to wait and see. In the meantime, the Boss has given us the day off so I suggest we tidy up here, and then go out and enjoy this unexpected holiday. We might even pop in the pub for a Sunday morning pint. We haven't been able to do that for ages." Thadius was already standing, the pile of books in his arms.
"Thadius Jonathon Williams, you amaze me, you really do." She shook her head slightly. Every now he'd surprise her, thankfully it was always a pleasant surprise.
He laughed. "It's called faith. He has his reasons for what he does and I for one am not going to stand in judgement of him. He's always led me the right way before, he brought me to you, didn't he. I'm not about to doubt him now." He pulled Gemma from the pew and gave her a quick kiss. "Now woman, are you going to help me or not?" He gave her a light slap on the bottom to get her going, but his hand lingered a little longer than necessary.
"Is that allowed in church?" Gemma laughed.
"Only when it's precipitated by love." He assured her.
They quickly gathered up the books. Thadius left the church doors open in case someone needed it while they were out. He always believed it wrong to lock the door of the church to the people but had to obey the diocese direction to keep the doors locked, but not today.

Thadius was upstairs changing his clothes when the phone rang. Gemma answered it.
"Ah, Mrs Williams, it's Mrs Chambers here. I was wondering if I could have a few words with your husband the reverend."

Gemma wondered why people always said that (your husband the reverend) as if she had two husbands and one wasn't a vicar. She felt tempted to ask her what she could possibly want with Thadius after what she had said the other day, but decided against it, instead she said. "He can't come to the phone at the moment, Mrs Chambers, can I take a message or shall I get him to call you back?"
"Can you ask him to come around, Mrs Williams. It's Marty; I'm very worried about him."
I did try to warn you, Gemma thought to herself. "I'll get him to come straight around." she said into the mouth piece.
"Thank you, will he be long, do you think? Only…"
"Ten minutes." Gemma promised.
"Thank you."
Gemma replaced the receiver. "Tad." She called up the stairs. "Mrs Chambers wants you to go around her house. She's very worried, something to do with Marty. Are you nearly ready?"
Thadius came to the top of the stairs, his shoes in his hand, he sat on the top step to put them on. "What's he done?"
"She didn't say. I said we'd go straight around there. I did try to warn her about him but she wouldn't listen." Gemma said to him as he came down the stairs.
"Probably ran off with the family heirlooms." He pulled on his jacket and they left the house.
"I don't think it can be anything like that." She said as she got in the car. "If he had stolen anything she would have phoned the police not you, besides she said she was worried about him."
They drove in silence, neither of them mentioned their spoilt plans.
Mrs Cambers was waiting at the door when they arrive. "Thank you for coming reverend. It's Marty, he's locked himself in his room and I can't get him to open the door. I heard him screaming." She gave an involuntary shiver. "I ran upstairs to see what had happened, I knocked on the door but he wouldn't answer. I could hear him crying asking Joshua to forgive him. I tried talking to him, to get him to open the door but he wouldn't. I'm really worried about him. I went back up after phoning you and I couldn't hear anything." She led the way upstairs and pointed to a room at the far end of the hallway.
Thadius knocked on the door. "Marty, it's reverend Williams, can you open the door." He listened for some movement. "Marty." He

called louder this time. He listened, his ear against the door, he thought he heard a whimper, whatever it was it made him feel uneasy. "Have you got a spare key, Mrs Chambers."
"No. can't you knock the door down."
He gave the woman a troubled look. He knocked and called again. Thadius found the silence more unsettling, he made a decision. It wasn't going to be easy theses old doors were pretty sturdy. He stood back and gave the door a hefty kick. The door didn't even shudder, all that he had achieved was to hurt his foot.
"Can I help?" Gemma asked.
"No, I don't think this going to work. Mrs Chambers have you got an axe or something?"
"Yes in the garden shed."
"I'll get it" Gemma said pleased to have something to do.
"I'll get you the key." Mrs Chambers went with her. They heard Thadius give another kick. By the time Gemma got back with the axe Thadius had made some headway with the door, He finished the job with the axe, put his hand through the door and turned the key. The room looked empty but his senses told him it wasn't. There was a smell not the smell of death, for he knew that well, this was a sweet sickly smell. He heard something, a moan or a laboured breathe, it made him move forward. It was then that he saw Marty on the floor behind the bed.
"Oh, god no." It was Gemma's voice that had expressed his thoughts.
"Call an ambulance." He told her.
"But…what's happened?" although the sight sickened her, she found herself mesmerised, expecting the answer to reveal itself to her stare.
Thadius stood in front of her, obstructing her view. He turned her around "Gemma ring for an ambulance." He shouted at her. His voice so urgent it broke the spell she was in. She fumbled for her mobile.
"Mrs Chambers get me some towels." Thadius ordered.
Mrs Chambers went to enter the room. "What's happened is he sick".
"No don't." Gemma tried to warn, but the woman pushed her out of the way. "What has he done?" she asked not understanding what her eyes were seeing.

"Towels Mrs Chambers, Now." Thadius ordered. She obeyed immediately.
"The ambulance is on it's way." Gemma told him. She watched as he tried to amply towels to staunch the flow of blood. Impossible, she thought, the panic returning.
Thadius worked on, talking to him telling him to hold on that the ambulance was on it's way.
She was relieved when to the ambulance arrived, so she could leave the room.

Chapter Sixteen

Ben opened the door to Gemma.
"Where are the children." She asked him as a greeting.
"In the garden feeding Matilda." Before he could ask her what was wrong, she was already down the passage, going into the sitting room. He pushed the door home and quickly followed her in.
She stood at the window watching her children. A smile pierced her face as the normality of seeing Laura and Luke both trying to tempt the tortoise with their half of banana first, just as she had loved to do when she was a child, the sight eased her troubled mind.
"Where's Thadius?" Ben asked quietly. It was obvious they had had a row; her red puffed eyelids looked raw against her stark white face.
"Jim not here?" she asked ignoring his question.
"He's gone for a drink." He noticed a slight sign of relief on her face. "You and Thadius had a row?" He asked directly.
"No." her creased brow showed wonderment at his question. "Oh, Ben, you wouldn't think it possible. How could anyone do that to them self." She was in his arms, her head tucked into his chest, tears damped his shirt.
Ben held her away from him so he could see her face. "Gemma, where is Thadius, what's happened.?" His imagination was running ahead of itself, taking unhealthy leaps of it's own making.
"Thadius has gone to the hospital with Marty. That's what I'm trying to tell you." She cried.
Ben sat her down and listened to her story, although he had trouble following it, as she jumped from place to place as hysteria took over, faulting her speech.
"So you're saying that Marty, while high on drugs, cut off his own arm." He asked incredulously, when she had finished her story, not quite sure that he had understood completely.
"No" her voice was more steady, as if having once told of the horror the mind regained some control. "He told Thadius that he had just injected himself, he removed the tourniquet and he could feel the drug burning through his vein. He said he realised that what he had done was wrong, that Joshua would never forgive him that he knew he had to get the drug out of his arm." Her voice faltered. "So…" she swallowed down her own sickness which her stomach was having

trouble containing. “so with his own hand, he tore away at his arm, using his own fingers as weapons, he tore into his own arm, tearing into the skin, tearing out his flesh and muscles.” The sight of his arm rushed into her mind. The white bones speckled red where pieces of flesh still hung, like an half eaten carcass after a pride of lions had feasted on it. The hand hanging untouched and somehow unreal at the end of it. Lumps of meat, his own flesh strewn on the floor, blood pumping from what remained of his arm added animation to the otherwise still scene.
She had to run, reaching the toilet just in time. She was still retching when there was nothing left to come up. She rested her head on the basin while she waited for the spasms in her stomach to subside. She flushed the toilet the turned on the basin tap splashing handfuls of cold water over her face.
She wished the memory could be purge from the mind as efficiently as the stomach. She pulled the towel from the rack to dry her face, it’s whiteness gleamed in her eyes.
Memory flashed back, returning her to the house.
“What do you want me to do?” Gemma had asked.
“Get another towel, I’ve tied off his arm with my belt, but he’s still losing blood.”
She went to the bathroom, to get the towel as she went back to the room she noticed Mrs Chambers sitting on bed in a bedroom at the far end, she was rocking back and forth, tears streaming down her cheeks. Gemma hadn’t stopped, she couldn’t go to comfort the woman, Thadius needed her.
As she entered the room she stopped, realising that she would have to go over to them and she really didn’t want to see Marty’s arm, or what was left of it, again.
She set her sights on Thadius and didn’t allow her eyes to stray, she just hoped that she didn’t step on anything squidgy. She handed Thadius the towel.
“I wish they’d hurry up and get here. I don’t seem to be doing any good here.” He wished he could do more for the boy. “Helps on it’s way Marty, it won’t be long, just hold on.”
A small sound came from him as if in answer.
Gemma automatically looked down at Marty, glad to see that the towel covered his arm. There was no colour left in his face and if she

hadn't heard the sound she might have assumed that he was already dead.
"Gem, go downstairs and wait for the ambulance to arrive." Thadius told her.
"But, isn't there anything I can do?
"There's nothing you can do here, just wait for the ambulance." Said Thadius.
His eyes had a haunted look about them and she realised that he was thinking the same as her. How could the brain go that crazy, that it allowed him, urged him to do such a thing to himself. The pain must have been devastating and yet he had still continued to tear himself apart. A shudder passed through her and she was glad to be leaving the room.
When at last the ambulance arrived Thadius had gone with Marty and she had driven Mrs Chambers to her sister who lived in Great Yarmouth before coming to Ben's.
She turned her mind from the memory, finished drying her face then went downstairs.
She joined the children in the garden and tried to forget.

Chapter Seventeen

Father Knight understood God's will. He knew what his fate held, he was but a tool in God's hand to be used to shape the future of the world. He prayed for strength, scared that he might not be worthy of God's faith, that he would let the Lord down.
All his life he had known that he was important, that one day God would have a special job for him to perform, but he never dreamt that he would be the chosen one to complete such an important deed as this.
He had been invited here to listen to Joshua's teachings, along with 3000 other clergymen, supposedly, because of the work he did with delinquent children but Knight knew God's real reason for sending him here.
It wouldn't matter what Joshua said or did, no one would follow him, no one would listen, for the world was too crazy now. These were the crazy years, where life no longer had any value. There was no justice, only forgiveness, which in reality was only Gods to grant, and so the people got away with murder. Even if they were unfortunate enough to be caught they were only sentenced to a few years in prison instead of having to pay for the life they took with their own life. Taking life was of little importance and if life was no longer sacred what else could be.
That was why God had sent Joshua, to prove to people, once again, that there was life after death. To prove that they would have to stand trial for their deeds on earth, only then, the judge knew the truth of what was in their hearts.
Knight knew that no one would understand what he had to do, just as they hadn't understood Judas, everyone believed that Judas had betrayed God as well as Jesus, which wasn't true. Jesus had to die, it was all part of God's plan. If Jesus hadn't died he couldn't have been resurrected and it was the resurrection that was important.
Judas was born to betray Jesus. So when the time came to do God's will, he had no doubts, he did it with a kiss. Knight's weapon was a gun. He could feel it in his pocket and it was as comforting as the bible in his hand and the crucifix that hung around his neck.
He had questioned the use of a gun, or at least his use of the gun. He hadn't touch a gun since his army days, nigh on thirty years ago. He

doubted his ability, for he knew the shot had to be instant death as now days doctor's could bring people back from the very brink of death, and two of Joshua's six disciples were doctors, so he'd have to be quick but accurate.
God had told him not to worry, that he would be there to guide him, that he had complete faith in him. As long as he got close to Joshua before firing, everything would be fine.
Knight gave one final prayer for strength and guidance. As he turned his attention back to Joshua, where he was speaking on the stage, he knew that the time was now and that everything would be alright.
He pushed himself out of his seat and made his way through the stalls to the centre isle, saying "Sorry" and "Excuse me" to his colleagues as he picked his way through their feet.
He couldn't help the sin of pride creeping into him, as he walked down the aisle, he was proud to have been chosen by God. Who wouldn't have been? He held his head high, a small smile played on his lips as he climbed the steps to the stage and walked over to Joshua. His hand cradled the gun in his pocket, it felt good, a part of him. He stopped within three feet of Joshua.
Joshua turned to face him. "It's you, is it, you're the one?" he asked.
Father Knight was a little shaken, he hadn't expected Joshua to know. Fool! He chided himself, of course he'd know, Joshua would know God's plan. "Yes I'm the chosen one." he said, as he pulled the gun from his pocket, removed the safety catch and held it up in front of him. There was a lot of shouting but Knight couldn't hear the words, he was only aware of Joshua watching him.
"You're not the one." Joshua laughed. "You're not the one." Joshua held his arms out to the side, allowing his whole body to become the target, mocking the priest.
Knight didn't understand. Why would Joshua say he wasn't the one when they both knew he was? His hand holding the gun began to shake, he tried to steady it with his other hand but it made little difference. He must shoot; he must shoot now before someone stopped him.
Joshua was speaking but Knight couldn't hear him, his words didn't penetrate his mind, only Joshua's eyes reached him. The halo light that took the place of Joshua's eyes burnt into his. Searing through his eyes and on into his mind.

He tried to blink, to close out the pain but his eyelids wouldn't move. Tears filled them, trying to give relief but it felt as if the tears boiled on contact, increasing the pain. He could feel them scald his face as they streamed down his cheeks.
Still the light from Joshua's eyes burnt into him, filling his mind with visions, visions that no living person, or soul, should have to witness.
He wanted to scream, just as the lost souls in the vision were screaming out their torture, but no sound issued from his open mouth.
He tasted cold iron and he knew that his now steady hand held the gun firmly inside his open mouth. Joshua was moving closer to him.
"No." somewhere deep inside Knight screamed out. His hand didn't listen being directed by some other force. His soul prayed "God help me." as his finger squeezed the trigger, sending him to meet his maker.

Joshua appeared in the sky that night to assure the people that he had come to no harm. He said that he was heart broken by the day's events. That it caused his soul despair to see how little people appreciated the miracle of life.
He proclaimed that, in the interest of mankind, as from today no gun or any other automatic weapon would work.
He said that in future, if man wanted to kill each other they would have to do it face to face and look each other in the eyes as they committed the sin.

So strong was the belief in Joshua, that people all over the world couldn't wait to prove Joshua's prophecy right. Thousands of people were wounded or murdered that night, by their own hand or by that of another, where they wanted to try it out before Joshua's miracle had the time to reach them.

Chapter Eighteen

Gemma and Thadius hadn't watched Joshua's appearance that night, they weren't interested in the outside world. They'd decided to have an early night after the strain of the day, both emotionally and physically drained.
Thadius had arrived home late afternoon. Marty had died on the way to the hospital and Thadius had to wait to talk to the police. He had gone straight in the bath. Gemma threw out the clothes he had been wearing.
They had both felt relieved when it was time for the children to go to bed, the strain of try to act normal in front of them had been terrible.
A little later, Gemma sat up in bed waiting for Thadius to complete his second bath, he still didn't feel clean. Gemma felt better after her reaction at Ben's house and she was now eager to talk about it.
She heard the water run away and a few minute later Thadius walked in with a towel over his head. He rubbed vigorously at his wet hair.
"Feeling better? She asked.
"Yes, although I'm not sure I'll ever feel clean again." He said, throwing the wet towel and his bathrobe on the floor and got into bed.
Gemma got out of bed and picked up the two offending objects in silence, having long ago given up try to get Thadius to change his ways. He was a slob, last thing at night, and if she had said anything he would only have told her that he'd pick them up in the morning, but she wouldn't have been able to sleep knowing they were crumpled on the floor.
"Why do you think Marty did what he did?" she asked as she climbed back into bed.
"I don't know, babe." He shook his head. "I was talking to one of the doctors and it seems that Marty's not the only one." Seeing the shock on her face, he quickly went on. "No, I don't mean they did the same sort of thing as Marty, what he did, thankfully, seems completely extreme behaviour. No, what I meant was that a lot of people seem to have driven themselves mad by not taking drugs they're addicted to."
"But why don't they go for help, why didn't Marty get help if he wanted to give up?" Gemma didn't understand addiction, she

enjoyed a drink and still smoked the occasional cigarette now and then but there was nothing she had to use.
"The doctor was saying that they used to get a few people like that, who had used hypnotherapy to stop smoking. He explained that a good therapist will ask, when you are under, if you really want to give up, if you aren't sure then they tell you to come back when you are. Some therapist don't ask and there can be bad reactions. Most people will just start smoking again within a day or two, others can't smoke even though they want to, they end up having panic attacks, asthma attacks all sorts of things. He said that's what's happening with drug addict only the effects are a lot worse."
"So what he's saying is that he thinks they've been hypnotised by Joshua?" it wouldn't have surprised her if Joshua had hypnotised everyone.
"Joshua wouldn't hypnotise people, why would he, choice is what religion is all about. No, I think they want to change because of Joshua, but…"
"But?" Gemma asked when he didn't continue.
"I don't know…I just think that maybe...maybe Joshua's coming isn't the best thing to happen."
"Boy you've changed your mind."
"No, I don't think Joshua's done anything wrong. I just think that people are finding it hard to accept the truth. I'm not talking about Marty, although that was tragic, but that probably had more to do with drugs. No, I'm talking about the way Ben was behaving the other day. Ben's never been like that before, I've never known him to be fanatical about anything, but the other day, well, if he'd been in the wrong company he could have been dangerous."
"What do you mean, Dangerous?" Gemma jumped to Ben's defence.
"Gem, you didn't see him the other day, he was obsessed and if he had been in company that egged him on, instead of talking him down, well there is no saying what he would have done. You read about people killing people in the name of exorcising the devil. I've never believed those sort of people to be anything but evil with no religious beliefs whatsoever, but people who use religion to give them power. But I know Ben to be a religious man and yet if we'd gone along with him that day, well yes, I could have seen him jumping on you in an effort to stamp out the devil."
Gemma shuddered "Never!" she said

“I hope I’m wrong, Gemma, I really do.” His word held no conviction.
“Ben would never think like that, it’s crazy.”
“You didn’t hear him.” Thadius didn’t like talking about Ben in this way but his behaviour had been niggling away at him since. It happened, it was as if Ben’s personality had completely changed and alright it hadn’t lasted long, but it had shaken him.
“Perhaps Joshua has been hypnotising people, changing them.” It had to Joshua’s fault.
“No, I’ve not changed in any way, have I?”
“No.” thank god she said silently. “But I had warned you about Joshua before you saw him.”
“I didn’t take any notice of that.” His words were out before he thought.
“Oh, thanks.”
“I didn’t mean it like that.” He gave a heavy sigh. “Can we continue this discussion in the morning, Gem, I’m really knackered right now?” Before she could answer he grabbed hold of her hips and pulled her down the bed so that she was laying down.
“Hmmm.” She murmured.
“You’ve got some hope tonight, darling, I’d have trouble raising a smile.” He told her.
Gemma laughed “But you are smiling.”
“No, honestly I want to rest my weary head on your boobs and sleep.”
She took him in her arms and snuggled down with him. He kissed her left breast and said good night.
A few minutes later he said. “A man could believe he’d died and gone to heaven being here like this.” Gemma started to giggle. “Stop shaking, woman, I’m trying to sleep.”
Soon there was only their breathing to disturb the silence and although Thadius had pleaded tiredness, he couldn’t sleep. He should have told Gemma about the AID’s test he had, on the advise of the doctor but he hadn’t wanted to worry her about it tonight, not after the day they had, he’d tell her in the morning, they wouldn’t know anything for weeks anyway, there’d be enough time for her to worry.

Gemma had no problems sleeping that night, she had her usual nightmare about Joshua, but it didn’t wake her. Her brain realised that reality held more terrors that any nightmare could conjure up, she slept until morning.

Chapter Nineteen

Mary Thompson sat at the cliff edge, looking down at the pebbled beach below. The vicar's wife and children were paddling in the shallow waves of the sea.
Mary wondered if she should have a word with Mrs Williams, about her parents, perhaps her husband could talk to them, make them realise how unreasonable they were being. The vicar seemed quite nice on the few occasions when he had spoken to her, at the youth club. She had expected him to lecture her about coming to church but he didn't even mention the church until Dawn, her so called friend, told him that Mary didn't go, he just smiled and said that if ever Mary felt like coming along, she'd be more than welcome, that was all, just an invite.
Perhaps she could talk to him? "No." she said aloud. Religion was the route of all her evils. Besides he was probably worse than her parents now, everyone had changed, gone through some sort of metamorphosis. She laughed at herself, she sounded like something out of a SF film where everyone but her had been taken over by aliens. But everyone had changed, she reminded herself, since Joshua arrived.
"It's so bloody unfair." tears pricked her eyes. I'm angry she told herself, but she knew deep down that she was sad and very scared. She had lost her parents and she missed them so much.
Her parents and she had always had a good relationship. She loved them, even liked them as people, which couldn't be said about many child and parent relationships, going by what the kids at school said. Her parents had always been easy going. They had their rules and regulations, but they could be lived with and there were limits to her freedom, but that was ok they stopped her running into situations which she was only capable of crawling in. She used those limitations as a safety net, where she could reel herself in when she got out of her depth. Secure also in the knowledge that the boundaries of those limitations would always be moved back bit by bit as he grew comfortable with the responsibility for herself and other, until the limitation ceased to exist.
Once or twice those boundaries had been drawn back in, like the time she had got a bit drunk, she had decided for herself the next

morning that she wouldn't be doing that again, she didn't like the hangover, but it had taken her a long time to push those boundaries back into line again.
All in all her parents were easy going, they expected her to behave to certain standard and as long as she was no real trouble, they got on. They were friends who trusted each other. Or they did , until bloody Joshua appeared on the scene that is.
Suddenly her parents had turning from normal, fairly well adjusted people into witch hunters, who's sole purpose in life was to protect her and her two younger sisters from all temptations.
They had never been a religious family. Her parents had married in a church and had them christened, but they had never gone to church on a regular basis, only attending ceremonies, weddings and funerals. So when her parents started talking about God, Mary had thought they were winding her up.
It was no joke, she was living it and she was terrified. Her parents were possessed, or at least obsessed, by Joshua and she was scared of what they might do next. It had started with her magazine, just an ordinary teen magazine. She was laughing at a letter she was reading on the problem page, her dad had asked her what she was laughing about so she told him. He snatched the magazine from her hand and started reading, she had expected him to laugh and read a couple out, emphasising the signed (One Direction fan) as he had done before. Instead he tore up the magazine, shouting at her, telling her that she wasn't to ever read such filth again, that if he ever found her bringing the devils work into the house again he would give her a good hiding. She had ran to her bedroom crying, she had never seen her dad so angry before, she was scared that he might hit her. No, the way he looked at her that night she had been afraid that he might kill her. She had tried talking to her mum the next morning, but her mum had sided with her dad, saying that the devils temptations were everywhere and it was their duty as parents to protect them from evil.
Since then they had destroyed all the devils instruments of evil, the television, computers, mobile phones, all their dvds, cds and players. Mary was surprised the devil wasn't lurking in the gas oven, but no doubt he would get there. This was no laughing matter, she reminded herself, no this was definitely no laughing matter.

This morning her dad had stopped her from going to school because he had found her personal development folder and had read the work they had been doing on S.T.D. and contraception. He said he wasn't sending her to a school that taught her to be a whore.
She had ran out of the house when her parents had started to tear up every item of her clothes that they considered obscene, clothes that they had bought for her or given her the money to buy.
A few weeks ago her dad might have joke about her forgetting to put her skirt on, and when she pulled a face at him, he would have said that he had belts that were wider than her skirt, then he'd say that he hoped that that half a yard of material hadn't cost him too much, her mum would have laughed and told her to take no notice, that she looked very nice. Now…now they were acting like some puritanical extremists.
She couldn't go home, she didn't know where she would go, but she couldn't go back. They might kill her if she did. You heard of people going crazy and killing their families and her parents were acting crazy.
"Don't be stupid." She told herself. They were her parents, they loved her, they wouldn't hurt her…but they weren't her parents, were they. They might look like her parents and their voices were still the same, but their minds their beings weren't they were alien, crazy.
They were the one's possessed by the devil and Joshua was the devil himself.
A sob escaped from deep inside. She didn't know what to do, she needed her mum and dad, but they were gone and she didn't know what she should do.
Her sobs were coming fast and furious now, she couldn't stop them, they were too strong for her to control.

Gemma watched Laura and Luke as they tossed pebbles into the sea. The sun was gloriously strong for this time of the year, so she and the children had taken the opportunity to play on the beach.
"Five more minutes, then we'll have to go home." Gemma warned the children.
"Oh mum, we don't want to go home yet." Luke was always the first to complain.
"Times getting on and we have to go." She asid.

“But we’re having fun.” Laura put in.
“Do you want to go home now?” Gemma threatened.
“We can stay by ourselves, we won’t drown or anything we can swim.” Luke argued.
Gemma answered by giving one of her looks and both children went into sulky silence. Gemma was sure it was supposed to be teenagers who knew everything, not four year olds.
She had enjoyed the afternoon on the beach. It wasn’t crowded, being too early in the year for holiday makers, there wasn’t many other people about and it was nice to listen to her children’s laughter and the sea.
She, like most people of the world, had given a sigh of relief when it was reported on the new that no automatic weapons would work, although there were crazy people in certain countries who had tried to fire their missiles in the hope that what Joshua had said hadn’t been true.
The world had lived too long under the threat of missiles and bombs, atom or otherwise, not that it really stopped anything. Men would always be greedy for power and would still fight, even if it meant they could only use their bare hands, but it was nice not to have to worry about the whim of some crazy dictator who believed himself to be some sort of god, who had the right to decide who should live or die.
Even though Gemma was grateful for what Joshua had done, she still felt uneasy about him. This very morning she had asked Tad who he would choose, between her and Joshua if he had to make a choice. Crazy, she knew, but she was still having nightmares about Joshua, only now they were getting more personal and she was scared that she might lose Tad and the children.
Thadius had laughed until he realised how serious she was. “I told you, when I asked you to marry me, that if you wanted me to leave the church I would.”
“Yes, but that is the church. I’m talking about Joshua.” She insisted.
“Joshua, whatever, look I will never stop loving God, that is just in me, just the same as I could never stop loving you. There would be no contest, you’d win every time.” He assure her.
She knew she was upsetting him by her constant persecution of Joshua but she couldn’t help it. She knew a confrontation was

coming, she didn't understand how or why but it was and she had to know that she could win.
Gemma called the children and helped them put their shoes on. She gathered up their belonging and climbed the steps up the side of the cliff. As she walked along the cliff to the church graveyard she noticed a young girl crying, feeling unable to ignore her she asked.
"Are you alright?"
The girl nodded, sobs racked her chest making her unable to give a verbal answer. Then she was shaking her head.
"You're Mary, Dawn Sharp's friend aren't you?" Gemma recognised the girl. "Look why don't you come back to the vicarage with us. I'll make you a cup tea." She pulled the girl to her feet. "I can give your mum a call and…"
"No, you mustn't phone mum." Mary stopped, changing her mind.
"Okay, I won't ring your mum if you don't want me to. Do you want to tell me what's wrong? I'm not saying I'll be able to help, but I can try."
Mary nodded and allowed herself to be led away. "I don't know what to do." She said almost to herself.
"Well come on, you can wash your face while I make some tea then when you're feeling a bit better you can tell me what has happened and we can see if we can work anything out."
"Will your husband be there?" Mary asked, worried.
"No Thadius is out doing his rounds, he won't be back till later, and even if he was I'd pack him off to his study." Gemma assured her
"Mummy, why is the lady crying?" Luke asked the question that both children were itching to know.
"Mary is just a bit upset." She told them. To Mary she said. "Subtle, isn't he."
Mary laughed although she didn't know why. She was already feeling better, perhaps she was overreacting.
Later as she told Gemma about her parents she realised she wasn't.

Chapter Twenty

Thadius stood on the doorstep of 26, Whitley Crescent and waited for someone to answer his ring. He wasn't happy about being here, he didn't like interfering in parent-child situations, unless of course the child was in some sort of danger.
He thought that Mary had the whole thing out of proportion and it would turn out to be no more than a normal argument about what she was wearing.
But Gemma's words still rang in his ears. He had said that he didn't see what he could do, after Gemma told him Mary's story.
"Well can't you go around there, talk with them, make them realise their actions are a bit extreme."
"Gem, the girl as probably got herself a bit hysterical over nothing, you know how teenagers argue."
"No, Tad, Mary is petrified, she thinks they've gone crazy. Their actions are extreme." Gemma had bought the whole story as gospel.
"Mary said herself that they would never hurt her. I'll take her home and have a word to them. She'll be alright."
"Oh, and you can guarantee that, can you, Tad? After Marty's behaviour the other day." When he hadn't answered she went on.
"Well I just hope that if ever Laura is that upset about anything that she feels that she needs someone's help, that they'll give her a bit more help than you're prepared to give Mary."
That was why he found himself on Mary's parent's doorstep. He wasn't sure that he could make them understand their daughter's fears, even if they were ill-founded, without alienating the relationship further, but he had to try.
"Oh vicar, er, what can I do for you?" The woman who answered the door said.
The resemblance to Mary was unmistakable, even though Mary's face had a stark haunted look from her crying, put colour in her cheeks and a smile on her face and she'd be the image of her mother.
"Good evening, Mrs Thompson, I wonder if I might have a word with you and your husband, concerning Mary" Thadius asked.
"Come in vicar. What's Mary done? She's completely out of hand I'm afraid." Mrs Thompson led the way into a brightly lit kitchen.

“Bob, the vicar as come to talk about Mary.” She told her husband, who was sitting at the kitchen table with an open bible in his hand.
“What’s she done, vicar? She ran off this afternoon before we could stop her.” Bob stood and shook Thadius’s hand.
“Mary hasn’t done anything wrong, Mr Thompson. My wife found her on cliffs this afternoon, she was rather upset.” Thadius tried to assure them. Mr and Thompson seemed quite normal, from the way Mary had spoken he had half expected to find they frothing at the mouth. The fact that the first thing they both asked was what had Mary done, made him wonder if it was just a case of a unruly teenager rebelling against parental guidance. Still Mary was very upset and that was unusual from what he knew of her, not that he knew her very well, having only spoken to her a couple of times when she accompanied Dawn to the youth club, but she had always seemed a nice happy, friendly girl. He decided he wouldn’t say too much about what Mary had said, he didn’t want to cause more trouble, but perhaps he could act as a mediator, explain that Mary was finding their new found religious beliefs a little hard to understand, he’d try to make them understand that youngster needed spiritual freedom, to be able to grow, and that the danger of not giving that freedom could turn her from religion for life. Thadius never said, turned from God, because he knew many people who loved God but were against religion.
“Put the kettle on, Val. Come through to the sitting-room vicar.” Bob led the way back down the passage to the room Thadius had earlier passed on his way in.
The two younger daughters were sitting together on the sofa. They stood up as their father and Thadius entered the room and made for the door.
“No, Penny, Emma, I want you to stay and heed the vicar’s words. He’s come to talk about Mary, to tell us the errors of her ways.”
The sisters didn’t utter a word but resumed their seats.
“You misunderstand, Mr Thompson, Mary hasn’t done anything…”Thadius could tell that Thompson wasn’t listening, so he turned to the sisters. “Hello girls, don’t worry, your sister isn’t in any trouble.” He gave them a smile as he entered the room.
For a moment they raised their eyes to look at him but quickly looked away again without saying a word. Their eye had that same

haunted look of Mary's. They were afraid, afraid of their father, but why? Why be afraid of their father.
Then he noticed the walls. "Oh, dear sweet Jesus." The word escaped him as his heart sank. The walls were strewed with snippet of the scriptures from the Bible in bold red lettering. He was sickened as he read them. They were obscene, although he would have never believed that anything from the bible could be obscene, these were. Every one was about sin, vengeance, ridding the devil and Hell. There was no word of God's love, forgiveness, compassion and hope. Taken out of context like this, the words broke his heart, but riled his soul.
"I've been writing them in all the rooms so the girl's won't forget them." Thompson said, mistaking Thadius's look of disgust for admiration.
Thadius now understood the children's fear, their haunted look. Thompson was a maniac, he read the Bible and his insanity spewed out these perverse demonic threats. "Mr Thompson, you can't leave these words here, they're…" Thadius could feel his face burning as he tried to control his anger.
"It's our fault, vicar," the man continued, not listening to Thadius. "Val's and mine. We were sinners. We allowed Satan into our lives, brought our children up in the Devil's doctrine. But Joshua came to save us, to show us the way, to show us the only way. The girls are finding it harder to follow the light, Mary more than the others. It's our fault, our sin bred into them. It's our duty, Val's and mine, to burn the sin out of them, , to save their souls. Where's Val with the tea?" he broke from his speech without drawing a breathe. "I'll just go and see what's keeping Val with the tea."
Thadius stared after him, his face agog, not quite believing what he had just heard. The man was completely crazy, dangerously so. God knows what he'd do to the children, if he left them here. Thadius's imagination frightened him.
He bent down to the girls and took their hands in his. "Will you come with me? I'm going to get you out of here, take you to Mary." His voice was soft and unhurried.
The youngest let out a stifled sob, her eyes darted to the direction of the kitchen and for a moment Thadius worried that they were more afraid of disobeying their father that staying with him. The elder sister nodded and got up pulling at her sister to join her.

Thadius didn't know what he was doing, he only knew that he had to get them out and away from their father. He was scared that the youngest girl would loose her nerve and start crying, but to his surprise, once up she ran ahead of her sister, silently to the door. Thadius wasn't used to this sort of thing and he expected at any moment for Thompson to come out of the kitchen and catch him making off with his daughters. What would he do? He couldn't reason with the man, reason was beyond his ability.
He couldn't fight the man, but he wouldn't leave the girls here alone, not for a minute.
He could hear Thompson talking with his wife, it was as if they had forgotten that Thadius was there, no that was crazy! He wasn't about to stop and worry about it now, the girls were out of the door and he followed, stopping to pull the door to as quietly as possible. By the time he reached the street the girls were already running.
"Penny, Emma, back here, the car." He called them back. He had the doors open by the time they joined him. "Lock your door." He told them as they clambered in the back. He locked his own door, started the engine and drove away before anyone could follow them.
Emma started crying in the back, Penny comforted her, telling her they'd be alright now.
What have I done? Thadius thought, as he drove the girls home.

"You've kidnapped two of the Thompson girls!" Inspector Cole's voice repeated Thadius's words through the phone receiver.
"Well I didn't actually kidnap them, they came with me by their own free will, it's just that Mr and Mrs Thompson didn't know." He had phoned Cole as soon as he got home. "They were scared, Dave. I couldn't leave them there. Thompson's gone crazy, if I had left the girls, their lives would have been in danger."
"Thadius, if you believed the children were at risk you should have contacted…"
"There wasn't time. If you had seen his eyes, Dave." Thadius had seen them, that look, the brilliance that shone through the eyes in expectation, that knowing that he could do whatever he wanted and no one could stop him. Because he was right. Thadius had seen that look before, as a boy and knew the meaning, it had haunted him then, it terrorised him now, but this time he was a man not a boy and he could stop it. Assured that he had taken the right action, he went

on. “I’m going back around to Thompson’s, Dave, see if I can talk to him, but I don’t want to leave Gemma and the children here alone, he might decide to come over here while I’m on my way to see him. Any chance of an officer coming over to stay with them.?”
“No, Thadius, you aren’t going anywhere. I’ll come over and talk to the girls, then if I decide there is cause for concern about their safety I’ll talk to Thompson. In the meantime…”
“Dave there is no meantime, Thompson is a time-bomb waiting to go off. He’s going to hurt someone, Dave, and he isn’t going to stop just because I’ve taken the girls, he’ll just change the name of his sacrifice.”
David Cole had been friends with Thadius ever since he had taken over St. Stephen’s and in all that time he had never known Thadius to go off half cocked about anything. If anything, Thadius always played down situations, but now he was talking about time running out and he was scared, the fear was audible in his voice. Cole bit his bottom lip as he decided. “Okay, Thadius, I’m coming over, then we’ll go to see Thompson together. If he is as crazy as you say, you won’t be able to do anything alone.”
“Okay, Dave, but hurry.”

Chapter Twenty One

David Cole had brought two officers with him, one he had left behind with Gemma. Thadius had quickly told Dave what had happened as he climbed in the back of the car with him.
As they drove, in silence to Whitley Crescent, Thadius couldn't help but wonder what scenes were taking place behind the curtain drawn windows, of the rows of quiet houses that they passed. Were the families inside touched, since seeing Joshua, by the deepest understanding of each other, feeling the warm anticipation of a new hope, peace and love for all mankind.. Only beginning to live, having taken God into their hearts. Knowing the lord's love for the first time.
Or did those curtains hide the insanities of the minds inability to except the existence of God. The reality twisting and breaking their mind, so that they couldn't hear God's words, accept his love. Instead of their souls being set free, their minds caged them in fear of demons. Making them seek out the devil in others, fearing it contagious, like some disease, allowing paranoia to take control until the mind believed the only protection from the devil was to destroy those whom they believed to be possessed.
Why people found it so hard to accept love, was beyond Thadius, accepting love was the easiest thing in life. Perhaps it was the responsibility that went with it, that they couldn't take. In receiving love, whether from another person, a creature or God, came the responsibility of trust, respect, honour and protection. What a small price to pay for the joys and pleasures of returning that love. Why couldn't people accept how easy it was, why did they have to seek out difficulties?
The car pulled to a halt outside No. 26.
"Let me do the talking Thadius." said Cole, before getting out of the car. Thadius understood Cole's attitude to him, he thought that Thadius had overstepped the mark and had put him in a bit of a predicament. But he hadn't met Thompson or seen the writing on the wall.
Thadius got out of the car and allowed the two policemen to lead the way.
"The door's open, Sir." P.C. John Barker told the inspector.

“I closed it when I left.” Thadius told him.
Cole pushed past the constable, pushed the door wide and took a step forward. “Mr Thompson, Mrs Thompson, it’s the police. Mr. Thompson are you there?” the house was silent. “Could have gone looking for the girls, I suppose.” He said when he got no reply.
Thadius hoped not. He should have stayed with Gemma, one policeman would be no match for Thompson.
“We’d better have a look around while we’re here. Thadius, which room?”
“The first one along.” Thadius was eager to get this over and done with so that he could get back home.
Cole stopped inside the doorway of the sitting room. Thompson had obviously had some sort of breakdown and he understood why Thadius was reluctant to leave the girls. “Obscene” was the word Thadius had used to describe it, malevolence was the feeling.
“He’s been busy this last hour, there wasn’t as many as this when I left and look his handwriting has deteriorated.” said Thadius, looking over Cole’s shoulder.
Barker joined them. “There’s no one in the other rooms, Sir, shall I check upstairs?”
“Yes. Oh, John.” The man stopped. “Any of this, in the other rooms?” He indicated the newly decorated walls. The constable took in the grim scriptures, shook his head. “Okay, John.” Cole waved him to the stairs.
Thadius stopped Cole from joining him. “Look, Dave all the photos have been removed from their frames, the girls said he’d only removed Mary’s.” Thadius hadn’t noticed the photos on his earlier visit, now he couldn’t miss them as Thompson had hung the empty frames back into place. Ten frames in all, six on the unit and four hung on the walls, all stared back empty at him.
“Sir, up here.” Barker called from the stairs. By the time they reached him, he was already radioing for an ambulance.
Val Thompson lay naked across the top of the stairs. She had been cut open from breastbone to the pubic; a horizontal cut just below her breast completed the deep bloody cross. Cole stepped over her body and followed the trail of blood that smeared it’s way to a bedroom.
Thadius sank to his knees, three steps below where she lay. “Is she dead?” he asked.

“A slight pulse.” Barker told him, but he knew she didn’t have a chance in hell.
Thadius brushed her hair back from her face, a silly thing to do in the circumstances.
Her eyelids flickered open in response to his touch, empty dead eyes stared at him. Her mouth began to move. “Why?” the word barely audible, just a sound in her laboured breathing.
Why try to talk? Thadius wondered.
“We…were… happy.” She persisted.
“Why…did…God…do…this?”
Thadius closed his eyes to hold back the tears that burnt. He had no answer to give her. When he opened his eyes again, Barker was closing Val Thompson’s eyelids and gave a shake of his head, as Thadius looked at him.
Barker stood up and followed Cole, leaving Thadius alone with the dead woman. Still in shock, Thadius said a prayer for the woman’s soul, then said a private prayer. He couldn’t help but wonder at the wisdom of the Second Coming, if so many innocents were to die.
In the stillness of the stairs Thadius became conscious of Thompson’s manic ravings.
“...don’t understand. I had to cut her open to release the devil. I had to do it, to save my daughters I couldn’t save their souls, while their mother carried Satan inside her, just as she had carried our daughter. I did it for them, don’t you see. I had to, to save…”
Thadius could listen no more. Sickened, he raised himself, wearily from his knee and went down stairs, out into the cold night.
He waited in Dave’s car, feeling ashamed and wishing for the first time, that he was anything but a vicar.

Chapter Twenty Two

David Lewis threw down the empty bottle of vodka and staggered from his chair to the kitchen where a plastic shopping bag stood on the kitchen table. He pulled out another bottle of vodka, he was celebrating. He had bought the bottles of vodka to drown his sorrows, but as he drank his way through the first bottle, his whole outlook on the future changed from one of anger, frustration and despair to one of excitement, hope and sheer pissing pleasure.

Alright, so he wouldn't be the one to bring Joshua to his knees, it was a disappointment, but he could live with that, just so long the bastard died.

He poured himself another drink, then held it up in front of him and said "Cheers." To a blown up picture of Joshua, that was taped to the wall next to his bulletin board. Not that there was much information on the board. There hadn't been much information to find on Joshua. Since the first day that he had met Joshua, a couple of weeks ago, was it only weeks? It seemed to David that Joshua had been taking the piss out of him for years, David had been trying to build a file on the man. So far, he had come up with very little, he had only been able to trace Joshua back for three years, then he had come up against a blank wall, and he meant blank. It seemed that Joshua didn't exist before.

He had arranged through his producer, along with just about every other T.V. station and newspaper in most countries, for a reward to be offered for any information on Joshua's childhood and younger years. Now usually you don't even have to ask. If someone appears in the newspaper or T.V. for any reason, you always had hoards of people crawling out of the woodwork with their stories of how they knew the person when he was still peeing in his pants at school. Everyone was willing to sell their own grandmother for the right price, which was usually cheap, it didn't even have to be money, for some the publicity was enough.

But not so with Joshua, no one seemed to have a picture of the man, no stories of him as a young man. Impossible of course, Joshua couldn't have just appeared from nowhere three years ago at the age of twenty seven. The man had to have a past, a discreditable one at that.

Still it didn't matter anymore, David reminded himself. Joshua would soon be dead. And to think it would be all Joshua's own doing. His death could be blamed on no one but himself, he may as well have put the rope around his own neck. Basically that's exactly what he done when he made all weapons useless.
David had been in the audience when that poor little priest had tried to kill Joshua, and that is what he had tried to do. Not that anyone believed David when he had tried to tell the world what had really happened.
It was the truth. David had seen the terror in the little man's eyes, when the gun he had aimed at Joshua turned, against his will, on to himself. David had seen the silent scream that didn't have a chance to emit itself from the priest's mouth as the gun pushed it's way in through the teeth.
Joshua had murdered the priest. Okay it was in self-defence, in a way, no one could blame Joshua for what he had done, and no one had because they didn't believe it. David couldn't prove anything, there had been no camera's in the hall, Joshua hadn't allowed them.
After the shooting David had rushed out to give a live report of what had happened. He had told the truth, told how the priest had gone on stage to kill Joshua and that Joshua had somehow managed to get the man to turn the gun on himself.
There was uproar, but more than that, the other reports gave a completely different version of what had happened, insisting that the priest had committed suicide and that Joshua had tried to save him.
David had been pulled through the hoops, these last few days, especially by his own company, who were expecting to have a slander case against them and were in no doubt that David would be done for slander. They had started their defence case by sacking him.
He had come home, to drown his sorrows but as he thought things through over an over again, he had realised Joshua's big mistake.
Joshua, for his own protection, had made it so that no automatic weapon's would work, obviously so that no other nutter could take a pot shot at him, but in the same process he had stopped every country form having any military power and no government would tolerate that. Joshua's days were numbered.
These people didn't need guns or bombs to kill, they had special ways of dealing with an enemy of Joshua's kind, not with a gun, not with a missile and it wouldn't be done with a kiss. No it would be

poison, a poison which could be administered just by Joshua coming into contact with it. Joshua wouldn't even know anything about it until he started to die of a heart attack or some other natural cause.
"Happy days." David said aloud.
"Celebrating. Are we?"
David turned around as he heard the words spoken behind him. To his amazement, Joshua was in his flat standing behind him. "What are you doing here? Fuck off out." David shouted.
"I've come to try to stop you from committing suicide, just as I did with the priest." Joshua told him.
David laughed. Joshua wasn't really here, it was an illusion. David could see right through him. He must have drunk more than he thought, he told himself. Some people saw little pink elephants; he saw a see through Joshua.
"Now, how would you like to die, by the rope?" Joshua asked smiling.
Before David could say anything, he felt a rope tightening around his neck. This was no illusion. His fingers clawed at the rope, to release it's pressure. Suddenly the rope gave way to his fingers and David fumbled to remove the rope from his neck.
"Not the rope then, I do wish you would help me, after all it is your death."
"Why are you doing this to me?" David croaked, his throat was bruised form the rope.
"You could always jump under a train or maybe jump off a tall building. Hey, do either of those grab you? No. I agree with you, there's no point in going out when we can stay here, in the comfort of your home." Joshua's words were soft.
"Why are you doing this?" David asked again, his bladder was in danger of emptying from fear.
"Perhaps a nice warm bath with a couple of razor blades?"
"You've made your point. I won't say anything else about you, not that any one would believe me now anyway. You have nothing to fear from me. Honestly." David pleaded.
"Fear, who is afraid? Pills are a nice easy way, but there's always the chance that someone's going to play the good Samaritan and get you rushed to hospital before you die." Joshua gloated.
"Then why are you doing this?" David had given up trying to control his bladder.

"Of course." Joshua smiled. "The knife, so precise, so clean. The knife."
David felt a red-hot fire tear through his guts. He cried out, not able to scream. He looked down to see his own bread knife plunged deep into his stomach. He tried to pull the knife out, just as he had pulled the rope from his neck. As his hands pulled on the knife, so the knifes serrated edge twisted in his guts. "Why?" David fought his agony, to make the word heard.
"You irritate me." Joshua told him before he disappeared, leaving David to die alone.

Chapter Twenty Three

Gemma worried about Thadius, he hadn't been himself since Val Thompson died. He blamed himself for her death and it didn't matter what Gemma said to him, he didn't seem to hear. She had tried telling him that he mustn't blame himself, that he had saved Emma and Penny from the same fate as their mother but nothing convinced him, he became more and more depressed, feeling that the responsibility stood firmly on his shoulders. Unlike Gemma, he placed no blame on Joshua, as far as he was concerned the blame was squarely at his door.

Over the last two days Thadius and Ben had been visiting the parishioner's homes, trying to talk them into returning to the church, Thadius believing that they needed guidance through these times, scared that more families were going through the same transformation as the Thompson's. They were subtly asking questions about their neighbours and friends at the same time, telling them that if anyone should have any confusing thoughts or any worries that they could call him or Ben about anything at anytime. Gemma knew they were wasting their time, no one would be returning to the church, even the social activities had been forgotten, no one came to the mother and baby afternoons, or the youth club now.

Both Thadius and Ben sat wearily in the armchairs sipping tea.

"It's strange." Ben said. "It's almost as if they've forgotten that the church exists. They seem surprised to see us, they are very polite, we've even been treated like long lost friends by some of them, but it's as if coming to church as never crossed their minds."

"Yeah." Thadius agreed with a heavy sigh.

"One good thing, though, they all seem to be normal, no signs of paranoia in any of them, they all seem to be going about their lives normally and their families seem happy." Ben said more cheerfully. He had also become very concerned when he heard about the Thompson's.

"Yes." Thadius gave a smile, his fingers rubbed at the worry lines that creased his brow. "Yes, they did, didn't they. Hopefully Marty and Thompson were the exception to the rule."

“Oh I don’t think you can class Marty and Thompson the same. I mean Marty had been using drugs for so long; there is no saying what he would have done at anytime. Thompson? Well, who’s to say how stable he was to begin with, you didn’t know him did you? It’s not as if he was a member of the church.”
“That’s true.” Thadius thought for a minute. “Neither was Marty, what if that’s the key? What if it’s affecting the people who had no religious conviction before seeing Joshua. There could be hundreds of people who are having problems and they wouldn’t ever think of coming to us.” Worry etched it’s way into his face again.
“There is nothing we can do, if there are. I’m not knocking on complete strangers doors.” Ben said with conviction. He had never gone uninvited to his congregation’s homes, until the last two day, unless someone was ill.
“I know.” Thadius realised that. “I just don’t want a repeat of the Thompson’s. I wish people would come back to the church.”
“They probably will.” Gemma said without conviction. “It’s early days yet.”
“By then it might be too late.” Thadius said almost to himself.
“Look, I’ll have a word with Bob Ward, get him to place an advert in his free paper, saying that if anyone needs spiritual help to contact us. It goes to most homes in the area. Mind you, they’ll probably think your trying to drum up business for yourself.” Ben laughed.
“I don’t care what people think. So long as no one else has to go through what Mary, Penny and Emma had to go through.”
“You did what you could, Thadius, you mustn’t blame yourself.”
“Yes, but it wasn’t enough, was it. I knew what Thompson was capable of and I did nothing to stop him.”
“Tad, I was the one who was concerned about them, but not even I believed that anything like that would happen. No one could have known, no one could have stopped it. You saved the girls, that’s what is important, you saved the girls.” Gemma was kneeling in front of him.
He patted her hand. “I know and you’re wrong. I’m not blaming myself, well not in the way you think. I just don’t want it to happen again.” He told her.
“It probably won’t.”
“No, it probably…” The phone rang interrupting him.

Gemma got up to answer it. She returned to the room a few minutes later. "Tad, that was the hospice. Mrs Brown's is asking for you. They said you'd better hurry." She said sadly.

"I'm sorry I haven't been in to see you, these last few days, Ethel, only…" He said as he looked down at her age blighted face.
"No, don't apologise, Thadius, you're a busy man and I'm grateful for you coming."
"So what have you been up to?" he asked. "And it's no good you asking me to smuggle you in a bottle of whisky again, the sisters a right dragon." Ethel had been suffering from terminal cancer for the past six months.
"I just wanted to thank you, Thadius, and say goodbye." She stopped him from saying anything. "You've made my life easier these last couple of months. You're a lovely man, Thadius."
"It's been my pleasure knowing you, Ethel." He placed a kiss on her brow.
"I must be dying, to get a kiss off such a handsome man." She laughed her eyes sparkled.
At that moment a woman rushed in. "Mum, why didn't you tell me you were so bad."
Thadius had heard Ethel talk about her daughter but he had never met her before, she didn't visit her mother very often. "I'll be outside if you need me, Ethel." He left the two women.
Mrs Brown died an hour later. Thadius waited to see the daughter. "Mrs Harris, I'm terribly sorry about your mother, she was a lovely woman. Is there anything I can do for you?" Thadius offered.
"No, thank you, reverend, my husband is coming to pick me up."
"Right well, I'll give you my phone number, for when you want to discuss your mother's funeral arrangements." Thadius passed her his card.
"Thank you, vicar, but I don't think that will be necessary, the crematorium will do that."
"Crematorium? But your mother wanted to be buried next to your father, Mrs Harris. They bought the plots years ago. On my last few visit with your mother, the service she wanted was basically all she talked about." Thadius explained.

“I’m aware of what my mother wanted, vicar, but a burial is completely out of the question. I don’t have time to keep coming all the way to keep her grave tidy. I’m having her cremated.”
“I don’t think tidying the grave is the important issue here, Mrs Harris, it’s seeing that your mother’s wishes are carried out the way she wanted them.” Thadius couldn’t understand her logic.
“It’s my decision, vicar, and I’ve made it, now I’m sorry if that spoils your plans, but.”
“Not my plans, your mother’s.” Thadius reminded her.
“Look, vicar, I’m not prepare to discuss this, you can come a say a few words for my mother at the crematorium, if you want, you’ll be more than welcome, but”
Thadius first reaction was to say no, but then he realised he’d be as guilty as Mrs Harris by not doing as Ethel wished. “I’d be honoured to speak for your mother, you’ll let me know when the funeral is taking place.” He held his card out to her again.
She took the car and gave him a nod then left.
Thadius stared after her. How could a lovely lady like Ethel produce a hard bitten woman like that.

When he told Gemma what had happened, when he returned home, she was as disgusted as he was.
“She knew what her mother wanted and still won’t do it.” Gemma couldn’t understand it.
“It’s not as if it has anything to do with the expense, which I could understand, if there is no money and you can’t afford it, then you can’t do it. But Ethel paid for her funeral up front. Still I was thinking perhaps she would give her permission for Ethel’s ashes to be buried next to her husband. That way Ethel would still have part of what she wanted, I’ll ring her in the morning.”
“That sounds a good idea, babe, surely she can’t object to that.” Gemma was pleased to see that Thadius was back to his usual caring self, instead of acting like a man who had given up.

Chapter Twenty Four

Gemma looked at her mobile again, still no signal. She tried the customer phone in the supermarket again, still engaged. She phoned his mobile, it went straight to voice mail, then tried the landline again. Who in earth could he be talking to all this time, fifteen minutes she had been trying to get through to Thadius so that he could pick her up, and all she got was the engaged signal.
Stop it! she told herself. She took a deep breathe and exhaled slowly. It was pointless getting angry, one of the children had probably knocked the receiver off and Thadius hadn't noticed, it had happened before while the children were playing. Thadius was probably waiting for her to call, wondering why she was taking so long.
She picked up the five shopping bags and made her way to the taxi rank. She wished she had brought the car, no she didn't, she wasn't safe to drive at the moment, her mind kept wandering she would have probably had an accident had she driven.
She checked through the shopping bags while she waited for a cab. She hoped she hadn't forgotten anything, but she probably had. She had wandered aimlessly around the shop longer that she had intended to, trying to think of everything she had to get. She wanted to be prepared, this time, if the hospital wanted to keep Laura in. Please Lord, she said a silent prayer, let Thadius and her be making a mountain out of a molehill, let it be something silly like a common cold. She knew deep down, they both knew that it wasn't, that it was Leukaemia, back with a vengeance. Why? why her darling little Laura, she had been through so much this last year, why did she and they have to go through it all again, weeks of…she closed her mind to it, she was getting ahead of herself. She fought to blink back the tears. Wait, wait until tomorrow, hear what the specialist has to say. She and Thadius probably had it all wrong, becoming paranoid about Laura's health, always expecting the worst.
A cab pulled in and the driver got out to help her with her bags. She gave him the address and was thankful when the driver drove in silence, the last thing she wanted, was to have to make small talk.
At first they hadn't realised Laura was unwell, being too concerned with other people to notice how quiet she was. It wasn't until he

started getting fretful and listless that they realised something was wrong.
It wasn't fair, it just wasn't fair. She remembered Mary Thompson using those words a week ago. Was it really only a week ago? It seemed like an eternity. She had meant to go over to their aunt's house to visit them, but she hadn't. Mary of course, blamed herself for her mother's death, and probably always would, believing, that if she had stayed that day, her dad wouldn't have gone berserk and her mother would still be alive. Five lives destroyed and for what. Thankfully there had been no other major crisis, or at least not that they were aware of, which was just as well, because she really didn't think that Thadius would have been able to take it. He had become morose sine Laura had become ill, it was as if every spark of hope had been snuffed out of him, taking his soul with it. She had never seem him so distressed before.
The cab pulled to a halt and Gemma got out of the car, she saw the back of Thadius's car turn the corner at the top of the road. Great he'd probably gone looking for her. She paid the driver as he put the bags at her feet, she picked up the shopping and went inside. A sense of loss poured through her for no reason. Stop it woman, pull yourself together, she scolded herself, they'll be back soon. She went straight to the kitchen to unpack the bags and saw the letter stuck to the fridge. With shaking hands she took it down.
Gem,
I tried to call you but couldn't and I can't wait for you to get back, I have to go. It's great news. Joshua is coming to England and I arranged for Laura to see him tomorrow. You realise what this means don't you, Laura will be cured, she won't have to go through all that pain again.
Wish you could be with us but this is too big an opportunity to miss. I'll ring when I find out more.
Love you
Tad.
Gemma pulled out her mobile and called his number, still no signal, she tried the landline but it took her straight to his voice mail.
"Damn you, Tad." she swore. "You haven't said where you are going, why couldn't you have told me where you were going"
Her voice sounded too loud, too brittle in the still silence of the house, making her more aware that she was alone.

She felt sick in the stomach, she felt as if she would never see the ones she loved again, which was crazy, where did that idea come from, she wondered.
Thadius would phone later, she hoped, and not leave it to the morning. Telling her that they were on their way home; they had seen Joshua and that he had cured Laura, just as he had cured the other children.
This thought did nothing to still the nagging that chewed away at her stomach. Joshua was going to cure her baby and instead of her being filled with joy and gratitude as Thadius was, the very idea filled her with fear and dread, the thought of that man laying a hand on her daughter made her flesh creep.
She walked into the sitting room intending to tidy away the children's toys, just for something to keep herself busy, but she stopped herself from doing so, scared that if she put their toys back into the box that stood in the corner of the room, that they may never be brought out again.
She had to top thinking like this, if she didn't she'd be ready for a nice padded cell by the time Thadius phoned.
She walked out the back door, down the side of the garden to the gap in the stonewall which led to the graveyard. She gazed up at the church as she made her way along the well-worn path through the headstones to the church.
She walked in. Thadius had left the church open since the Sunday that no came to the service. No one had walked through those doors since, no one seemed to have any need for the church now, except Tad, Ben and herself. Even the cleaner had stopped coming. Thadius had phoned her the first day she hadn't turned up, thinking that she was ill, she wasn't, she just said that she wouldn't be coming anymore.
Gemma did the cleaning now, not that it got very dirty, it was more of a case of keeping down the dust that grew hungrily like mould on a over ripe strawberry.
It was strange, the way people had left the church. She understood they might feel they didn't need the church for spiritual guidance now they had Joshua, but they had also stopped attending the social events that the church ran. It wasn't as if it was anything that Thadius had done, people still held him in respect, were pleased to see him when he visited. It was just the church itself, as if it no

longer existed and it wasn't just their church, it was the same in every church in every parish, not only in England, but world wide in every religion.
As she walked down the centre aisle, she became aware of a feeling of great sadness, deeper than any grief. So strong was the atmosphere that she stopped in the middle and took a slow look around the church, expecting it to have changed in some way. It remained the same in structure, it only felt different.
Gemma had never experienced any religious commitment, she wasn't even sure that she understood religion, which was strange considering the only two men she had ever loved, live their lives by religion.
Not that she didn't believe in a God, she liked the idea of a supreme being, retribution, having to reap what you sow, she just didn't understand blind faith, belief.
She had always loved churches, all churches but especially St. Stephen's. She always felt comfortable in church, as soon as she walked through the doors she felt as if she was wrapped in a blanket of peace and serenity, a voice whispering, that only her soul could hear, unheard words soothing and yet inspiring, telling her that everything was possible, nothing impossible, a haven in a cold world. Today there was only sadness. For the first time in her life she felt the need to pray.
She sat in the front pew and looked up into the crucifix that stood behind the altar.
"Dear Lord…" her voice sounded small in the emptiness, making her conscious of her own voice, as if hearing it for the first time. She felt embarrassed but went on, clearing her throat first. "Dear Lord…I know I'm being silly, but I'm scared…scared that something bad will happen to Thadius and the children- I know nothing bad can happen from them visiting Joshua, but, I have this feeling, that something…I don't know. Thadius was terribly excited, perhaps he won't be concentrating on his driving-No, Tad would never endanger the children by doing something like that. I don't know…but please keep my family safe. Please…I know I shouldn't be asking, that I should have faith in your decision, satisfied with your blessing on mankind by sending Joshua to us, but…"
A coldness seeped through her. She tried to ignore it, but the coldness bit deeper. She felt her hair rise as one by one every pore in

her skin closed in an attempt to stop the icy tentacles burrowing deeper.
A darkness fell around her. She looked up at the church window, it was still light out there, not as bright as it had been for evening was drawing in, but still to light for the shadow that fell.
She shot up from the pew, turning around in the same movement, expecting to see someone, something behind her. The church was empty but for her. Empty and yet there was a new feeling of malevolence, so strong that she expected the walls to shake in anger. The coldness, the shadow still clung to her. She wrapped her arms around herself trying to still the shudders that convulsed her body.
"I don't understand!" her voice echoed, she started edging back. The felling was coming from the church itself, impossible, but true. The church itself was changing it's atmosphere, she had been aware of it as soon as she walked through the doors. "But why?"
Something touched her bottom as she took another step back, she swung around, there was nothing sinister, just the altar behind her. She looked at the crucifix, feeling that she had been called.
It started to glow, distorting the hard straight line of the cross, softening the structure into an essence of warm yellow, white light.
"Oh dear God…" It was no more that a whisper. "It's wrong, isn't it? It's all so bloody wrong." She was running, out of the church, into the street.

Chapter Twenty Five

By the time Gemma reached the London Road she was gasping for breath, she had to stop, she cursed herself, while her body regained it's natural rhythm.
She started to walk, while her chest still heaved. Darkness was beginning to fall too quickly. The road was quiet, unusually so for the A12, giving her a sense of unreality.
She was glad when she reached the five cottages, which were the only houses this end of the road, lights from the open curtains helped her feel less alone. As she came to the last cottage she noticed that Mrs Taylor wasn't in her usual place at the garden gate, she was always there until the early hours of the morning no matter the weather.
Gemma hesitated, looked up the weed overgrown path, should she knock? Just to check the old lady was all right. She walked on deciding that Mrs Taylor probably didn't feel the need to stand guard any more. Her nightly vigil had been in fear of UFO's landing and taking over the world. Joshua's appearance probably assured her that he was protecting us from the Martians now.
The local children called her a witch and knowing the tales of the road being haunted by the hounds of hell, they would only walk this road to test their bravery. Gemma herself had walked along there when she was young, enjoying the thrill of the ghost stories her friends told as they walked the long dark road.
Mrs Taylor was a bit strange, an eccentric to say the least, but completely harmless. Gemma wondered what people would call her if they knew what she believed Joshua to be, crazy, insane or just another harmless oddball.
She started to run, walking this dark lonely road made her feel a little nervous, the ambience was spooky and the sound of shoes slapping the pavement added to the eeriness. She found herself wishing for traffic.
A screech shattered the stillness of the night. Gemma welcomed the bird call from the wild life park, soon she would see the lights of the first Kesingland pub, returning to civilisation and nearing Ben's cottage.

Gemma reached Ben's cottage, heaving for breath, she gave the knocker three hard raps, waited a moment then repeated the action. The door opened. Jim stood with a paintbrush in his hand, white gloss daubed his hands and clothes. "Gemma." His voice held surprise at seeing her.
"Where's Ben?" she gasped, as she made her way down the passage.
"Mind the door, it's still wet." He warned her as he followed her in.
"Ben's out but he shouldn't be long, he's supposed to be helping me finish this off." He indicated the freshly painted sitting room.
"Where's he gone? I've got to find him."
"I don't know." He told her. She looked upset and she turned to leave. "Wow, calm down." He stopped her from leaving. "You might as well wait, he won't be long. Sit down, tell me what's wrong." He wiped his hands on an old rag, went to the dresser and poured Gemma a whiskey.
"Tad's taken the children and I don't know where they've gone. I need Ben to find them for me." Her eyes pricked with frustration.
"Thadius has left you?" Jim found that hard to believe. He hadn't known them long, admittedly, but they seemed happy enough.
"No, Ta hasn't left me. He's taken Laura to see Joshua and I've got to stop them. Only he didn't tell me where they were going. He arranged it through the church. I need Ben to find out where they are."
Jim put the glass of whiskey in her hand. "Here drink this, it'll calm you down. If you're that concerned why don't you just phone his boss, the deacon or bishop or what ever he's called?"
"Are you joking I'd have more chance of getting information out of the mafia than the church. They won't tell me, no one supposed to know that Joshua is coming to England tomorrow, well except the church. They'll just tell me that they'll get a message to Thadius to phone me." She took a large gulp of whiskey and shuddered as it burnt her throat.
"Well what is wrong with that? You could get him to ring you here." Jim suggested.
"No, that's no good, I need to see Tad face to face. His letter sounded so excited about Joshua curing Laura, that I'm not sure I will be able to talk him out of it over the phone, I'll have a better chance if I see him. Besides I want to be there so that

if he doesn't agree I can get the children away." She drained the glass, appreciating the warming effect of the liquid on her body, he muscles were beginning to relax already.
Jim refilled her glass. "I don't understand. You're saying that Thadius has taken Laura to meet Joshua so that she can be cured, but you want to stop it from happening, but why, it's the best thing that could happen, isn't it?" Jim felt he had missed something along the way, surely Gemma wanted her daughter cured. "It's good isn't it.?" He asked her.
"No it's not good. It's all bloody wrong." She took another swig of whiskey. She needed to think, how was she going to convince Ben to help her. His opinion would be the same as Jim's, if she failed to use the right words he wouldn't help her, believing her to be crazy, like a Jehovah's witness refusing a blood transfusion to her dying child. She had no time to think, she heard the key being turned in the lock. Before Ben was in the room, she was telling him what had happened.
"Oh, Gemma, that's great news." He gave her a big hug. "I'm so pleased for you. What an honour, hey, and to think you'll never have to worry about Laura again. These children that Joshua cures are blessed, you know, blessed for all time." He hugged her again. "I really am pleased for you, Gemma."
"Ben, you don't understand, we've got to stop it. We've got to find Tad and the children before Joshua can get his hands on them."
"What!"
"Ben, Joshua isn't what he seems, he's evil, Ben." Gemma tried to explain.
"Gemma, how dare you, I won't listen to such blaspheme in my house."
Gemma realised she was handling this all wrong. "I'm sorry, Ben, I'm not trying to make you angry. I need your help. I know I don't understand a lot of things about religion, Ben, but that isn't important, what is, is that I'm a mother fighting to save her children's lives, so please hear me out."
Ben said nothing, he just glared at her with a look that she hoped wasn't hate. She finished her drink and watched as Jim refilled it.
"I'm no different form anyone else, Ben. Don't you think I'd like Joshua to be what he is supposed to be. I want a hero, just like everyone else. Someone who rights all wrongs, who'll bring some justice to the world, who'll show us how easy it is to love. Yes I

want an hero, just like everyone else. And what did we get, Joshua, white charger and all." She couldn't keep the venom from her voice.
"Now you look here, you. . ."
Ben tried to complain, but Gemma cut him off. "I've never understood pure faith, I always thought that faith meant that if there was a second coming you wouldn't need miracles to recognise him, that you'd be able to tell who he was just by looking at him, that you'd be able to see the purity of his soul, the love in his heart, with just one look at him. I've always known that I'd never be able to do that, how ever much I tried, I'd need miracles. I'd need to see him walk on water, to prove who he was. As it goes I needn't have worried, Joshua has miracles coming out of his ears. It's almost like a show, he's giving us everything that we expected, but it isn't right, you must feel that, Ben It isn't right."
"But people did recognise him, just by looking at him, Gemma. Lots of people were converted when they saw his face in the sky." Jim said. He hadn't been himself, nevertheless a lot of people were.
"Exactly, but only because he appeared in the sky. When they had seen his face on the T.V. and in the newspapers they didn't believe in him, it took miracles for them to believe. You, Ben, you weren't convinced until Joshua appeared in the sky."
"Yes, I know I wasn't convinced until then, that is my failing, but that proved who he is." Ben didn't understand why her feeling were so strong against Joshua. She had always had strange ideas about God, her views were completely romanticism on the whole subject, but even then they were half hearted, no more that whimsical notion.
"What did Joshua's appearing in the sky prove, Ben, that he was different from us mere humans, that he had abilities to do things that we can't even understand? But that does make him the son of God. As far as I can see, people don't even think about God now, only Joshua. No one wants to know the church anymore, people don't seem to have that happy contentment from their beliefs as you an Tad have always had. He's not what he seems, Ben, it's all wrong."
"Gemma." The disbelief echoed in his voice. "The way you speak, anyone would think that you believe Joshua to be some kind of alien or something." Ben laughed aloud.
"It doesn't matter what I believe, Ben, Joshua can go on doing what he likes, I don't care, but at this very moment Tad is waiting to put

Laura into his hands in the morning and I can't allow that to happen, Ben, he's evil." Her voice had risen to almost a shout.
"Gemma, you're overwrought and you've drank enough of this." Ben took the glass from her hand. "Now go home, go to bed and tomorrow when Thadius and the children return home, you will feel better. You should be rejoicing, Gemma, Joshua is going to cure Laura."
"So why do I feel as if I'm putting my baby into the hands of the beast." Tears pricked at her eyes in despair. She agreed with Ben, she shouldn't have drank so much whiskey, her head felt fuzzy, when she needed it to be clear. She needed Ben's help, but all she had only managed to alienate him toward her. She had done everything wrong. "Ben?" her voice was soft, sad, as if she knew she had lost. "Have you tried thanking God for Joshua? I did this evening. I ignored my gut feeling, Laura was going to be cured and I was thankful, so I went into the church, to give thanks. God and the church didn't like it."
"Gemma, you have been an atheist all your life, you can't expect to get answers from the church because it suits you." Ben said.
Gemma felt anger rise in her. "I may be an atheist, Ben, but at least I'll listen to God when he tries to talk to me, you don't, you don't want to hear, you don't even want to know what he thinks because you already know it all." Ben's face turned red. "Ben, please, listen to me as a father. Forget religion, the church, God, after all everyone else has." The words were out before she could stop them. "Ben, please I need your help, I'm begging you to give me that help as a father, out of love, as a father who thinks his child is making the biggest mistake of her life but will still help her, out of love. You don't have to believe in my reasons or anything like that all I'm asking you to do is find out where Tad has gone, please Ben, I've never asked anything of you before, please." She picked up the glass and finished off the whiskey. Ben didn't even look at her, he stared at his hands.
"I'm sorry, Gemma, you're wrong and…"
"Forget it Ben, it doesn't matter, I'll find Tad myself." She pushed herself up from the chair and immediately wished she hadn't. The room spun around fast, making her feel nausea. She shouldn't have drank the whiskey, she had eaten nothing all day and the drink had

gone straight to her head. Her legs felt weak and the floor was rising to meet her.
Hands held her. Voices came to her as if from a distance.
“My fault, I’m afraid. I thought the whiskey would help relax her.” Jim apologised.
“Well it’s done that that all right. Put her in my room.” She heard Ben say.
She felt herself being picked up and carried. “No. I’ve got to help Tad, I’ve got to find them.” She protested but she had no power to struggle. God help me, she pleaded as she sank into oblivion.

Chapter Twenty Six

"Gemma, wake up. Come on, we've got a long journey in front of us." Jim put a cup of tea on the bedside cabinet. "I've brought you one of my shirts, will that do you?"
Gemma opened her eyes to see Jim standing before her. She was about to ask what he was doing there, when the memory of the night before came flooding back to her. "What time is it?"
"3.30, you've got fifteen minutes to get washed and dressed and into the car." He told her.
"Ben's found out where Tad's gone. Where is he?"
"Ben was on the phone for a couple of hours last night. They're in Porthbeor, Cornwall. Get up." He made his way to the door.
"Jim," he stopped "What made Ben change his mind?" she needed to know.
Jim shrugged his shoulder. "He went to St. Stephen's after you passed out. When he came back he started ringing around. Then got about four hours sleep. We're leaving in fifteen minutes, if you're not ready we leave without you." He smiled at her.
"I'm there already." she promised. "and thanks." She pushed back the duvet and Jim left. Ignoring her heads protestations, she ran to the bathroom. Ten minutes later she was downstairs. "Thanks Ben." She kissed him on the cheek. "You went to the church, you saw the crucifix?" She asked excitedly.
"What do you mean? I saw the crucifix?" he asked, suspicion appeared on his face.
"The cross, it didn't change? Then why did you change your mind about helping me?" she didn't understand.
"I'm a father who's helping his daughter even if he does think she's making a mistake." The coldness in his voice was evident as he repeated her words.
"Thank you." She kissed his cheek. "Please don't be angry with me. You taught me, as a little girl, to stand up for what I believe in even if it would be easier to go along with the crowd."
Ben grunted, then smiled. "Come on, we had better get started, we've got a long drive."
"Shouldn't we phone Tad first get him to wait for us?" It seemed the best idea to her.

"We can't, I wasn't able to find out where they were staying, only the venue; we'll have to find them there." Ben explained.
"Oh…Oh well, I'm sure we'll have no trouble finding them, once we're there. Thanks Ben."
"Are you two ready? We'll take my car, it's faster than that rust bucket you call a car, Ben." Jim pretended not to notice that Ben wasn't amused. He could see this was going to be a fun trip.
Jim tried to make small talk as he drove, telling little stories about times when he had been here before, anything in fact, so long as it couldn't be turned around to Joshua. It was hard work as Gemma and Ben had little to say. After an hour he gave up, turned on the iPod and allowed the music to fill the silence.
Gemma wished she had had time to get something to eat before they left, her stomach was empty and sick. She wasn't sure what it was that contributed to her sickness more, hunger, last nights whiskey or fear. Fear of not being able to talk Tad out of Laura's cure, afraid that that she may be completely wrong, that her sanity was out of balance and that because of her Laura might die. No, she was sure, sure that removing Laura from Joshua's reach was the right thing to do. Not for rational reasons, because she didn't have any, apart from the fact that it wasn't normal to dream of a complete stranger only to find out that the man is a new messiah, but that wasn't her reason. There was no reason, just feelings, intuition, instinct what ever you choose to call it. She knew that she couldn't allow Laura to go through with the cure, if she did, it would become completely out of her control, running into something that she had no knowledge of, only fear. It wasn't easy convincing people that you were right, when reason was stacked against you..
Gemma had no option, her compulsion was too strong, she had to get her family away, the why was unimportant. Reason, she assured herself, was the curse of mankind. Birds didn't look for reasons when the urge to take flight came, they flew away in a mass from their territory, leaving behind the earthquake or some other natural disaster to follow, knowing they could always return when the danger had passed.
Although knowing that she was doing the right thing, Gemma's fear grew with every mile they travelled. She felt like a fish that had taken the bait, she was hooked and slowly being reeled in, she only hoped Joshua wasn't the one at the end of the line.

Did he know of her existence as she knew the truth about his?
“There’s a service station coming up, I’ve got to fill up with petrol, do you want to stop for something to eat?” Jim asked them, cutting into their thoughts.
“We can get some sandwiches from the petrol station shop, no point in stopping longer than we have to.” Ben suggested. He also felt tense, feeling a need for urgency for them to get there. He had spent the past few hours wondering what Gemma had meant when she asked him about the cross. There had been nothing different about the cross, had there? Perhaps he had been too perplexed by the atmosphere of the church to notice. The church had been in his care for thirty years and he had never known it to have such a feeling, it was explosive with sadness and anger. He had sat in a pew for an hour trying to make sense of it, he had never believed the building itself to have any influence over the spirit of the church, believing that it came from God alone and if that was true, was God sad and angry? If that were true, why? He didn’t try to make out that he understood any of it, but he did understand Gemma’s fear. That was the reason he was making this journey with her.

Chapter Twenty Seven

When they arrived at Porthbeor, the place was packed solid with cars. They had to park the car and walk the last couple of hundred yards. As they reached the bay, a man came over to them.
"You won't be able to get down there. The police have cordoned it off. They say there's too many people down there already." The young vicar informed them.
"Thanks, but we were invited." Ben told him, then walked over to where the police were guarding the steps that led down to the beach. A few minutes later he rejoined them. "We can't go down to the beach, but they said that if we go along the cliff we'll be able to hear Joshua from there." Ben was excited. The thought of seeing Joshua in the flesh had driven all other thoughts from his mind. He strode ahead of Gemma and Jim, eager not to miss anything that Joshua had to say.
"He's talking to them from the beach?" Jim said rather baffled.
"How am I going to talk to Tad if I can't get down to him?" Gemma said. The dread that had been rising on the journey turned to panic. She hadn't considered not being able to get to him once she arrived.
"Let's take a look. Ben might see someone who can sort things out." Jim told her as he walked swiftly on. He didn't really think there was any possibility of that happening, but like Ben, he was eager to get a glimpse of Joshua.
When Gemma joined Ben and Jim and looked down on the people she was filled with despair. There were hundred's, maybe a thousand people on the beach in the small bay. Their faces turned to the sea, as if awaiting the arrival of a ship.
Then she saw what they were watching. Joshua was standing in the sea, or to be precise, he was standing on the sea. The tide was gently breathing in and out along the shore, but Joshua's figure remained stationary, the waves having no effect on his stance.
Well that answered the question of why on the beach, Gemma muse. She found him pathetic. It was like a theatrical performance; in fact, the whole scene seemed familiar.
Nausea struck, as she realised where she had seen this scene before. It was her dream, the nightmare that had been haunting her over the last few weeks. As she looked around she even recognised some of

the people who were sitting in the audience. She couldn't see their faces but she knew that they would all be smiling, in a trance like state, as they listened to Joshua. She had seen their faces, seen their smiles and she had seen them burn. It was defiantly her dream, only real and this time her family were among them.
She started to scan the crowd below, her sight flicked from row to row in search of one head. Thadius where are you? She mentally called him. She wasn't even sure he was there, they might have been turned away, just as they were. No, Tad was down there with their children, she could feel it, but where? Her head began to spin in panic, sweat started to run down her forehead. Where are you, Tad? She told herself to calm down, she had probably missed them in her panic. She took a few deep slow breathes to calm herself, then she started her search again only this time slower, row by row.
She felt panic rising again as she searched half of the crowd, without a glimpse. Then she saw them. It was Luke, she spotted first, he had started to run up the aisle and Thadius had to pull him back. They blurred as tears of relief filled her eyes. They were there.
Now all she had to do, was to find a way down there. She looked back along the cliff to the steps, but immediately dismissed them when she saw three police officers guarding them. There had to be another way down a path or something. She looked for the easiest way down the cliff. Further to the right there appeared to be a pathway, albeit a steep decline, it was obvious that others had gone down to the beach by it, so she could, just as long as she kept her balance.
Slowly she made her way down, holding on to rocks where possible, to keep herself steady, she wasn't very good at climbing, she always expected to fall.
Less than half way down the decline became more abrupt, adding speed to her momentum until she felt her feet running away with her. She tried unsuccessfully to regain control, but she lost her footing and went down on her bum. She grabbed at rocks as she hurled by, in an effort to break her fall.
Her hands screamed out in pain as the weight of her body tore the rocks from her grip. Using her feet and hands she slowly brought herself to a stop.
She sat for a few moments waiting for her legs to stop shaking, her hands were torn and bleeding and her whole body ached.

She wanted to stop, to stay where she was, feeling too scared to go down or up. She could wait until someone came to rescue her, she told herself. She would have given anything to just be able to sit there and cry, but she couldn't because Tad had brought their children here and she had to get them out. She cursed him.
She started to make her way down, against her body's protests. "Just let him say I'm being stupid." She warned aloud as she continued down the cliff on her bum. Eventually the path levelled off a little and she was on her feet again. This time she didn't worry about falling, she just wanted to get down the bloody thing.
When she reached the bottom she stopped and tried to get her bearings, it all looked different from down here. Eventually she worked where she was and made her way to Thadius.
This was going to be the hard bit, convincing Tad to leave. There wouldn't be much time for discussion because she didn't know when the burning would start. He'd just have to trust her. Did he love her enough to trust her? She could have answered that question without doubt a few weeks ago, but now… people seemed to change once Joshua got hold of them.
She tried to listen to Joshua's words, needing to remember when, in her dream, the burning started. It was no good, his words meant nothing to her, she hadn't listened to him in her dreams.
As she listened to him now, she was surprised to hear the mockery in his voice, his every word seemed derisory, couldn't the people hear him laughing at them? From the loving look on their faces, she gathered not.
She found Thadius and the children, and bent down to give them a hug.
"Mummy." Laura shouted her surprise.
"Gemma, what are you doing here?" Thadius asked in surprise. "I've been worried sick about you. I've been trying to phone you and Ben all morning, but there seems to be something wrong with the phones. I suddenly realise I hadn't told you where we were going and I knew you would be worried. What have you done to your hand?" Thadius took her hand in his and examined the cuts, then looked at her face. She looked terrible. Dirt smudged her cheeks, emphasizing the paleness of her face. She looked tired, that if he hadn't known better he would have thought she hadn't slept for a week. He pulled Luke onto his lap. "Move up, Laura, let your mother sit down."

Gemma didn't move. "We've got to get out of here, Tad, now!"
"Laura hasn't seen Joshua yet, it's been arranged for us to see him after." Thadius explained.
"Thank God for that. We have to leave now, Tad, there isn't going to be any after. This is my dream, my nightmare, we have to leave before the..." She couldn't bring herself to say the word, as if by voicing it she would make the burnings start.
"But, Gemma, that was just a dream, it can't..."
"Tad, why do you think I've come all this way to find you? We have to go."
"But what about Laura?" he asked.
"We'll have to take our chances."
"Gemma, your dream could be wrong. If we wait to see Joshua, we won't have to talk about Laura's chances, there will only be certainty."
"Yes, certain damnation for all of us." Gemma watched Thadius turn back to Joshua and she feared she was losing him. "Please, Tad, you have to trust me."
He turned to look at her, not knowing what to do. Her green eyes looked larger than he had ever seen them before and they were full of fear, like a trapped wild animal who's only expectation was death.
"Okay, we'll go." He smiled
Gemma stood up, relief washed over her. Then she realised that Joshua had stopped talking. She could feel his eyes boring into her back, she turned to see him staring at them.
Thadius must have seen him also, for she suddenly heard him say "Move." She could hear his fear in that single word.
She scooped Laura into her arms and made her way to the back of the crowd.
She noticed the face of the people as she passed, they were still watching Joshua, but in their mesmerised state they hadn't even realised that Joshua ha stopped talking. With the fixed smile on their faces, they had a look of insanity about them.
"Which way?" Thadius asked taking hold of her arm.
"I don't know. I thought we'd be able to go up by the steps but that's impossible."
She pointed to the steps, which were packed with people.
"How did you get down here?"
"I found a cliff path, but it's too steep. I almost fell, coming down."

“It’s the only way. Come on show me where it is.” Thadius could still feel Joshua’s eyes burning into his back. He knew they had to act fast before Joshua somehow stopped them.

Chapter Twenty Eight

"We won't be able to climb it, not with the children." Gemma said despondently, as she looked up the cliff, it looked a long way.
"We will, we've got to. It will be a lot easier going up than coming down." Thadius could see that she still wasn't convinced. "Unless you want to stay?" he asked.
"No."
"Give me Laura; you'll be able to climb better without her."
"No, I'll take her. I'll be alright, you take Luke, he's heavier." She needed Laura in her arms. She knew she wouldn't give up until the children were safe.
"Fine if you're sure you can manage. I'll be right behind you if you need to pass her over. Laura, hold on tightly around mummy's neck." He wrapped Laura's legs around Gemma's waist. "Ready?"
Laura started to cry, having picked up the unknown fear she felt from Gemma. "I don't want to go up there. We'll fall." She cried.
"We won't fall." Gemma tried to laugh to still her daughter's fear.
"It's easy, Laura, I could climb it by myself." Luke, who was always sure of himself, told his sister. He never saw any danger in anything and because of this he was extremely sure footed.
"I'm sure you could, but you're staying where you are." Thadius told his son. To Gemma he said. "Take your time." Although his instinct told him to hurry.
"Granddad Ben and Jim are waiting for us at the top." Gemma told Laura who had buried her head into Gemma's neck.
"Will he stop us from falling?:" Laura asked, big tears welled, ready to trickle from her big blue eyes.
This time Gemma laughed naturally. "He won't need to. I won't let you fall, we'll be up the top in a few minute." She promised.
Thadius had been right, it was easier going up. As the cliff got steeper she used the rocks for leverage. As they came to a bend about halfway up, she had to slow down to be sure of her footing. Suddenly something hit between her shoulders blades pushing her forward, the force digging the rock she was holding deep into her hand, she cried out in pain as it bit into her flesh.
"It's Joshua, he's trying to stop us. Keep going." Thadius spoke from behind her.

"But, why, why is he doing this to us?"
"I don't know. Just keep going." Thadius pushed her on.
Gemma turned around to see Joshua still staring at them, he was smiling, that same smile that had always sickened her. She turned back to Thadius just in time to see a rock smash into his shoulder.
"Tad!" she reached out for him.
"I'm alright, just keep going, we can't stop." He pushed her on. That had been the third rock to hit him and although Joshua wasn't literally throwing the rock at them, Thadius knew that Joshua was responsible for the rocks hurling themselves at them.
He turned the bend and realised they were halfway up. Thankfully, the attack had made Gemma move quicker, with any luck they would get to the top before they could be badly hurt.
As if Joshua had read his thoughts and decided otherwise. Stone and bits of rock started raining down on them from above.
He reached out for Gemma and Laura, he had to try to protect them. Gemma had stopped and was holding her arms above her to try to ward off the rocks. He was within two feet f them. He reached out his hand and almost touched Gemma's arm.
A rock hit his head, above his right eye, sending him reeling, nausea rose into his throat. He wanted to call to Gemma, for her to help him, but couldn't, only a groan emitted from his mouth. He turned to her, hoping that she had seen what had happened, but he couldn't see her, his eyes wouldn't focus, his vision was a red blur. His eyes stung with the blood that trickle in from the wound on his head.
"Daddy." Thadius heard Luke scream from far away, but that was wrong, he told himself. Luke should have been with him. He tried to clear his head, fight his confusion, but blackness gathered before his eyes. He fought to hold on to his consciousness, he couldn't black out, Gemma and the children needed him. He felt his strength drain from his body, his legs buckled under him, he tried to straighten his weakened knees but couldn't.
"Tad!"
His name being called was the last thing he heard as he sank into a black void.

"Tad!" Gemma shouted. She had turned, when she heard Luke scream, to see Thadius swaying, fighting to remain standing. Blood covered his face, his eyes stared unseeing, his dark brown hair

streaked red with blood. She reached for him, but as she did so he started to collapse, falling away from her hand as it moved close. Her hand was grabbed by small hands. She had forgotten Luke in her attempt to help Thadius. Luke clambered into her arms like a baby monkey climbs onto his mother.
She watched as Thadius fell to the ground, in what seemed like slow motion. A rock wedged his arm and body, holding him safely on the path.
Both children were crying.
"Is daddy going to die?" Luke asked.
"No." Luke's words brought her out of her trance. "No, when we get to the top, we'll get someone to help him." She told them. At least the rocks had stopped raining down on them, she thought.
She couldn't believe no one had seen their plight, why wasn't Ben or Jim coming down to help them? She gave one last look at Thadius, knowing there was nothing she could do for him while she was alone with the children, his only hope was for them to get to the top and get help.
"You both hold on tight." She told the children unnecessarily, as they were both holding around her neck so tightly that she felt she was being strangled.
Her pace was slower now that she was holding Luke's weight as well. She faced the cliff, needing both hands to pull her way up the path.
A rock hit her leg, on her calf muscle, sending a burning pain shooting up her leg into her back. She clenched her teeth so as not to cry out. Ignoring the pain she moved her leg, testing it's support. It felt strange, as if it didn't belong to her, numbed and yet burning with pain, but it held her weight. She climbed on. Have to reach the top, she told herself.
The rocks were coming fast and furious now that she was the only target left. Most, luckily only skimmed her arms, shoulders, hips and legs as she carried on climbing.
A rock hit squarely on her back, forcing the air from her lungs. She cupped her children's heads in her hands before they smashed into the cliff. She screamed out as her hands were crushed between the cliff and their body weight.

Why was he doing this, why was he trying to kill them? They only wanted to leave, they weren't hurting him, so why was he doing this?
She felt the last of her reserve and strength drain away. She couldn't go on, she wanted to drop, to sink into oblivion, just as Thadius had.
"Tad, I'm sorry, please forgive me but I can't..."
"Gemma, Gemma hold on we're nearly there" Ben called.
She looked up to see Jim and Ben coming down the cliff to meet her. She would have cried with joy had she any strength left.
Jim took the children from her arms and with them went her last ounce of fight, she started to fall to the ground. Hands held her up, through a haze she heard Ben talking.
"Jim, get the children out of here. I'll take care of Gemma."
Hands pulled her up the path, rocks still hurled at her but Ben used his body to shield her from the blows.
"I'm sorry, Gemma, for doubting you. I thought he was...well he obviously isn't." Ben said.
"Help Tad." Gemma pleaded.
"Thadius is alright. I've got to get you out of here first, Joshua is still after you. Why is he doing this to you, Gemma?"
"Because I know." Gemma said, although she wasn't quite sure what she meant by it. They had reached the top of the cliff and Gemma collapsed to the ground.
Her whole boy screamed out for her to stop. Her exhausted mind wanted to close itself to the pain of her bruised and broken body. She had to stop.
"Because you know what, Gemma?" Ben asked.
It was warm and cosy, the place she had gone to.
"What do you know Gemma? Tell me what you know."
Ben was shaking her. She wanted him to leave her alone, to the warmth, to the nothingness, but he wouldn't. He continued to question her, shaking her.
"I know he's not who he says he is...He can't be the saviour." She dug the words out from deep inside her, just so he'd leave her alone. She tried to sink back into the nothingness, where she didn't need to feel or think about anything.
"Gemma, how can you know for certain, why can't he be the saviour? Gemma, you have to tell me." Ben repeated the question over and over again, shaking her all the time.

She wanted to hit him, to knock his hands from her, but she couldn't because she didn't have the strength. In the end she shouted at him. "Because I am."

Chapter Twenty Nine

Those three words released something in Gemma that she never knew existed. Whatever it was, took over her physical and mental being, giving strength, motive and serenity where before the had only been exhaustion.
She stood up, there was no longer any pain. Her hands, as bloody and swollen as they were, felt no different from how they had felt all her life.
She walked to the edge of the cliff. Joshua was waiting for her to appear. Seeing her he smiled.
"I thought it was the man." He laughed. "Devious."
"No, it's me." She assured him.
Their words were spoken softly, but were heard clearly by both.
"You shouldn't have come." He warned.
"I had no choice." Gemma answered truthfully.
"You can't win." He told her.
"We'll see."
"The man," He motioned to Thadius. "is of the church, so you know how many followers your father has." He mocked. "Not many, not anymore. Their souls are mine. All over the world, they are praising me and my father."
"The people believe you to be God's messenger. Their souls still belong to him."
"Yes, strange creature, these people. They only hear what they want to hear. They believe that when I talk of my father, I talk of God. They haven't even realised that they no longer think of God, they only think of me. I expected it to be easy, but…When I told my father my plan he didn't believe it would work, he didn't believe they could be fooled so easily." He laughed. "All it took was a miracle or two to win all those souls. It was so easy." Joshua boasted.
"And of course by healing the children, you fooled everyone." Gemma added.
"I like children." Joshua said simply.
"Don't try that with me. I'm no fool. You cured the children because they were no use to you dead. You can't claim the souls of children, only adults."

"There is that as well, but don't sound so superior, we only did the same as you."
"Not quite. I didn't lie."
"You've controlled things for centuries. Now it's our turn."
"Never! I'm here to stop you."
Joshua laughed with true humour for the first time. "Allow me to remind you. Power comes from the souls you own and I won them all…" He stopped, his attention strayed for a moment, when he returned his gaze back to her, his eyes were sparkling.
"I see you're not alone." He mocked.
Gemma turned to see that twelve strangers had joined her along the cliff. "There has always been thirteen of us, waiting for you to come."
"It's not enough."
"More than enough, for you Joshua. The people will soon forget you and return to the churches."
"Never. They belong to me and there is nothing you can do to stop me."
This time Gemma laughed. "They are my father's, they belong to him."
"No." Joshua looked amongst the crowd of followers before him. He needed to know for certain. He choose a number of people at random, then returned his gaze to Gemma. "We'll see, shall we?" His smile was back in place.
A soul searing scream filled the still air, Gemma immediately recognised the icy shrill and knew that soon the air would be violated with the smell of burning flesh.
She could see Joshua grinning, mocking her, knowing the effect the burning were having on her.
She had to stop him. She screamed "No."
A white warm light shot from her open mouth, heading straight for Joshua. Within seconds it was entwined with twelve other lights, merging together into a spinning ball of light.
It spun in the air, gathering strength, then stopped, before hurling itself at Joshua's chest.
It picked Joshua up, without slowing it's speed, carrying him further out to the deeper waters of the sea, before it dived into the sea, pushing Joshua down before it.
Gemma collapsed on the ground.

Chapter Thirty

The light shone bright red against her eyelids her heartbeat quickened in fear. She opened her eyes instantly, expecting to see a ball of light closing in on her, waiting to engulf her in flames.
Her eyes slowly focused on a window, where the morning sunlight shone brightly through.
"Gemma, it's good to see you back with us, you have had us all worried. I'll get a nurse."
She turned her head, Ben was sitting in a chair next to her bed, she realised she was in hospital. "No, wait. Where's Tad, is he alright?" her throat felt thick and numb.
"He' fine. He needed a few stitches in his head and they kept him in hospital overnight, but he's fine now. He'll be back soon, he's taken the children to get something to eat. It's you, that we've all been worried about. You've been unconscious for three days." Ben told her.
She looked down at her hands they were both bandaged.
"Your hands are nothing to worry about, they're a bit messed up but no bones are broken." He assured her when he saw her looking at them.
She moved her fingers, unsure, but they didn't hurt at all. "Gemma, can you ever forgive me for doubting you? I had no idea…well who would have done…I.."
"Shush." She rubbed his hand. "Joshua, is he dead?"
"Yes, his body was washed ashore yesterday."
"Does anyone know what really happened?
"No, you needn't worry. People came out of their trance just in time to see him hit by a fireball. Everyone thinks it was a freak storm. They believe it to have been ball lightening that struck some of the people in the audience, catching them alight, then it hit Joshua. Of course there are those who are saying that it was a fireball sent by God because Joshua was a fraud."
"How many people burnt. Ben?
"Don't you worry yourself about such things." He tried to ignore the question.
"How many, Ben?"

"There have been reports from all over the world of people burning to death in unexplained incidents. They died about the same time as the people on the beach. But that doesn't mean that it had anything to do with Joshua." Ben knew that Gemma wouldn't believe that for a moment and wasn't surprised when he saw tears rolling down her cheeks. "Gemma, don't cry, it wasn't your fault, you saved us all, you destroyed…"
"Yes, yes I remember." She interrupted him. "I just hoped it was a dream."
"I don't understand. You are…did you never know who you were until on the cliff?" Ben asked.
"It wasn't me. It had nothing to do with me…I was used."
"But.."
"No, Ben, It had nothing to do with me. I'm just me, Gemma, wife of Thadius, mother of Laura and Luke." Her eyes pleaded.
"Don't worry about it." Ben said. He could see that Gemma was too distressed to discuss it now, so he didn't go on. "I'll go and find Thadius for you."
A few minutes later Thadius rushed in, happy to see her awake. He sat on the bed
Beside her and kissed her. "Am, I glad to see that you're alright." He let out a heavy sigh. "You've really had me worried."
"I'm sorry, babe, but I'm fine now. I just want to get home."
"Well let's wait and see what the doctor has to say, hey."
"I'm fine, Tad, really I am. What about you, your poor head." She reached up a hand to touch the plaster. "I thought you were going to die."
He kissed her. "It's nothing." He assured her. "Just a couple of stitches. It's you, I've been worried about. Look, I've got grey hairs now." He laughed.
"And the children, are they alright?" she asked, they had been so upset.
"Yes, and they'll be a lot happier now that they can see you're better. They were upset for a day or two, but they're okay now. Ben will bring them up in a minute. Oh, and Laura's either had a miraculous recovery or we were panicking over nothing. I had the doctors here, check her over." He smiled.
"Thank God for that." Gemma sighed.
"Gem?" The smile left his face.

"Yes."
"While I was on the cliff, after I had passed out, I came to and I thought I saw you at the top talking to Joshua and…did it really happen, or was it concussion?" He had seen it all.
Gemma took a deep breath. "Does it matter?" she asked.
"No…yes…I don't know." He answered honestly.
"It was the concussion." She said a little too quickly. Seeing he didn't believe her, she went on. "Tad, whatever happened, was nothing to do with me. I was used and I'm not very happy about it, but it won't ever happen again. I'm me, just me an I want to get home so that everything can get back to normal. I'll even be nice to Mrs Chambers from now on."
"Can anything be normal again? He asked.
"Nothing has changed, Tad, nothing." She put her arms around his neck and pulled him close, she needed his closeness.
He put his arms around her and hugged her to him, a little too tightly for her bruise back, but she didn't complain, she felt too good.
He kissed her. "No, nothing has changed." He agreed. He held her at arms length, looked into her eyes and smiled. "Oh, and it doesn't matter. I've always known you were a very special lady."
Gemma started to smother him in kisses, she was so happy, knowing that she had nothing more to fear.
"Hey." He said laughing "are you trying to get us thrown out?"
"Yes. Let's go home, Tad."

Made in the USA
Charleston, SC
06 June 2014